NORANDIA

MIGUEL TRUJILLO FERGUSON

NORANDIA

Acknowledgements

I would like to extend my gratitude to my friends and family members who have helped me bring this book to life.

This book is dedicated to

my Grandmother, Nora

Author's Note

I take pleasure in writing, so after travelling through different countries and contemplating their beauty, I thought of writing a fictional story in the hope of captivating the reader. This story is based in medieval times, where kings and queens ruled the lands while living in marvellous castles. While these times may be familiar to us, the landscapes are unknown, for the story happens in a world which doesn't exist. Furthermore, I should let you know that the names of the characters in my tale have been purposely chosen for their meanings. These names also provide insight into their personalities.

I chose the name *Norandia* because of my grandmother, whose name was Nora. She played an important role, not just in the life of her two daughters, but also in the lives of her four grandchildren. She taught us good values while taking care of us. We enjoyed and lived many stories together.

The name Nora, which is of Irish and English origin, means to honour, to be highly valued or esteemed, and because the names in this book have been chosen for their meanings, it seemed fitting to call the kingdom Norandia.

CONTENTS

Prologue   13

Chapter 1   17

Chapter 2   21

Chapter 3   27

Chapter 4   31

Chapter 5   41

Chapter 6   45

Chapter 7   49

Chapter 8   59

Chapter 9   65

Chapter 10   71

Chapter 11   75

Chapter 12   79

Chapter 13   83

Chapter 14   87

Chapter 15   95

Chapter 16   97

Chapter 17   103

Chapter 18   111

Chapter 19   115

Chapter 20   125

Chapter 21   129

Chapter 22   131

Chapter 23   133

Chapter 24   137

Chapter 25	141
Chapter 26	145
Chapter 27	149
Chapter 28	155
Chapter 29	161
Chapter 30	165
Chapter 31	173
Chapter 32	181
Chapter 33	187
Chapter 34	191
Chapter 35	195
Chapter 36	199
Chapter 37	203
Chapter 38	207
Chapter 39	209
Chapter 40	213
Chapter 41	217
Chapter 42	219
Chapter 43	229
Chapter 44	233
Chapter 45	239
Chapter 46	243
Chapter 47	247
Chapter 48	255
Chapter 49	257
Chapter 50	261
Names and their meanings	265

PROLOGUE

The wind had slowly been picking up, whispering its deepest secrets into the ears of the young warrior. He was sitting by the seashore watching and listening to the waves crashing against the coastline, a sound that brought him peace and relief. His eyes were closed.

When he opened them again, he fixed them on the sea, observing in the distance a misty cloud advancing towards him.

The wind hadn't lied.

Could this work to my advantage? He thought.

His reflections were more like a mumble, but nobody heard them, for there was no one nearby. Yet, unheard though they were, they brought him comfort. He knew that Benjamen, the king of Norandia and his adversary, had gathered all his troops to put an end to a dispute which had been going on for too long. He was moving towards the coast followed by his captains, horsemen and seven columns of a thousand soldiers, each well-armed.

The land had suffered much since the young warrior had been away; the green pastures were no longer visible, the trees were withering from the drought, crops were destroyed, fishing boats had been left abandoned by the seashore, and the dry terrain cried out for attention.

These were all things that with time and much hard work could be restored. However, the young warrior was concerned about the villagers from the land, for they seemed unhappy, with little desire to carry on living.

Now all that was about to change.

Yosef, who had been a knight for the king's father, approached the young warrior. "It's time to move," he said.

The warrior thanked him. Without delay, he stood up and called Tytus and Kislon, also knights who had left honourable positions to serve him, and another soldier who was holding a white flag.

"Mount up!" he shouted.

The men climbed onto their horses and headed behind the young warrior towards Benjamen.

Even though Benjamen had acted savagely in reducing the kingdom to poverty, he still had an iota of honour. When he saw the white flag, he chose three captains to accompany him, and galloped towards the warrior and his men to find out their petition.

"Benjamen!" the young warrior called out.

"What do you want?" Benjamen shouted.

"I am here to claim …"

The young warrior did not complete his sentence.

"How dare you!" the king yelled. "Are you not ashamed after being the author of our father's assassination? Listen, I will be merciful. I will allow you to leave in peace, on the condition that you never return."

"You have mistaken me for a coward," the young warrior replied. "No, I won't leave. In fact, I want what was meant for me."

"Fine!" Benjamen made it clear he didn't want to hear anymore. "Prepare to die. All of you!"

"Wait! Why should unnecessary blood be shed?" the young warrior cried. "Let the fight be between us, just you and me, over there" the young warrior pointed to the seashore. "The winner takes the crown."

Benjamen stroked his chin and looked at his captains. After a few moments thought, and receiving a nod from them, he grinned. "You have just signed your death warrant!" he said.

The young warrior stared at Benjamen's black armour. It was bulky and covered in spikes, making him look like a demon from hell, intent on dragging his victims into the underworld. His helmet had two small black horns sprouting from the forehead. A few inches below were his eyes, windows to his soul. They were ablaze with hatred.

Following not too far behind their black-clad king were his five captains, keeping their distance as they approached the beach. They stopped sixty feet from where the two men were to fight.

The young warrior's armour was lighter, but the grey, silver and golden patches of the metalwork shone with such a brightness that they would have brought light even into the darkest abyss. His helmet had a longitudinal crest of short, red, horsehair - symbol of aggression and a sign that the young warrior would never lose hope, even in the face of the worst evils.

The young warrior now stood alone. Tytus, Kislon and Kristal, his armour bearers, remained at the stipulated sixty feet, their troops just beyond.

Both men faced each other. The world stood still. Silence reigned for a moment. All eyes were upon them.

Benjamen looked to his left and counted the young warrior's followers. "Are those the only men you have?" he sniped. He blew air from his nose as he chuckled.

"No!" the young warrior retorted with a smile, relieved to see Seff and the rest of his soldiers positioning themselves behind Benjamen's troops. "There are more of my soldiers behind yours."

"Enough!" Benjamen said, drawing his sword. "Fight!"

1

Many moons ago, a prosperous kingdom called Norandia achieved great honour by negotiating peaceful treaties and by standing firm against all attempts to invade its lands. Its royal rulers had gained respect from the neighbouring kingdoms over the course of generations.

The king's castle was situated on a hill and from it the whole territory could be observed. The castle was considered the heart of the kingdom which, from there, extended towards the north, east, south and west. Fortresses had been built on its borders and, with them, the walls that protected the kingdom.

On every corner of the castle there was a tall tower with a conical roof which established the castle's perimeter. The only tower which stood out was the one in the middle, for it was square and taller than the rest, used by the watchmen to detect any incoming visitors. This tower had a long pole with a blue flag which waved when the wind blew, having in the centre a golden eagle with its wings spread wide as it rested on a white mountain peak. Behind its large brown body there were two golden swords in a cross shape pointing downwards. This was the emblem of the Kingdom of Norandia.

Beyond the northern walls stood a range of tall and wide mountains which protected the inhabitants from any direct invasion. From these mountains flowed a small river which travelled along the fields to feed the lake found at the north-eastern side of the kingdom. The rich vegetation around this lake was of many shades of green, and this gave a sense of vitality, surrounded as it was by a variety of bright and colourful flowers. To ensure that the kingdom had plenty of water, the previous kings had sunk numerous wells which were spread all over the kingdom. All this added to the richness of the land.

The king of Norandia was called Staffan, a tall and robust man with short dark brown hair and a ducktail beard. He was known by all his villagers as a righteous and caring king. He had many friends but also, like all kings, he had enemies, even some who wanted to kill him. To counter this threat, Staffan had established a new law in Norandia; all villagers, both men and women, when they reached the age of eighteen had to join the king's army for four years. After that, they were free to go back to their homes, on the condition that if the king ever needed them again, they would comply. Everyone in the kingdom therefore knew not only how to cultivate the land. They knew how to fight.

The king's wife was a compassionate and loving woman who supported her husband. Her eyes were possessed of a deep tenderness, but when necessary, they could appear grave. She had light brown hair and brown eyes, and always dressed elegantly. Her name was Ysabel.

Even though the times were peaceful, the king had to be prepared for any circumstance, and due to that, he made sure that he had a powerful and well-equipped army led by several trustworthy generals. The soldiers were prestigious warriors, but the king knew that he couldn't just rely on his own men, so he placed a notice in all the villages appealing for strong and skilled fighters. Many came forward, but after several tests only eleven were chosen, eight men and three women who were loyal to each other and to the king and would fight shoulder to shoulder with him.

These weren't just ordinary people; they were the king's personal knights, and to differentiate them from regular soldiers their armour was silver. Each of them came from a different village, and this was shown by wearing a certain colour patch on the back of their helmet, right shoulder and shield. Each of these knights was responsible for training their own young apprentice, who with time and preparation would become the king's knight. The knights lived in the king's castle, remaining close to him all the time.

In the summer, there was always more movement than usual, and that was because on the west side of the kingdom there were many boats of different shapes and sizes, all in constant transit. These weren't just arriving with products from other kingdoms. They bore the fish they had caught in the sea. When the port became full and no more boats could dock, they were forced to lie at anchor offshore, a challenge for the port's guards who were tasked with managing the safety of the harbour and the traffic of the boats.

Once inland, the people commenced trading. It was hectic; some were shouting their prices, others were trying to bargain, and others agreeing a sale. The moment the money was handed over, the buyer took his purchase and placed it in his horse's cart and drove off to the village from which he had travelled. In this way, food was collected and sent to the different hamlets within the kingdom. To ensure the transit was smooth and no carts would obstruct the pathways, sentries patrolled the different roads.

The mornings were, without doubt, the busiest time for traders, but for those who lived and shopped there, they were part and parcel of a normal day. Besides buying their produce, the inhabitants would socialize and find out how their neighbour was doing.

"Stewart, your tomatoes don't look fresh today."

"What are you trying to say, Guillaume? I picked them myself this morning!"

"I have my doubts. I was hoping to do a deal with you but…" Guillaume scratched his head, "I will go elsewhere."

Stewart stroked his grey beard. "Come on, give me an offer."

"Ten tomatoes for this piece of fresh fish." Guillaume lifted the fish from his bucket.

"Really? Are you lacking fishing skills or something?" His mouth was open in amazement. "That is a small fish. Five of my juicy tomatoes and I call that a fair deal!"

Guillaume bit his bottom lip. "Deal!" He nodded and stretched out his hand, waiting for Stewart to do the same so that they could shake in agreement, sealing the trade.

Among the fishing boats there were several vessels carrying the king's soldiers who were patrolling the sea ready to reject any unwanted visitors. On occasions, people had tried to come into the kingdom as an excuse to sell new products, but in the end, they just brought problems within the villages. So only those with official papers were allowed entry.

Winter was different. The markets were quieter and there wasn't as much going on because the weather was only favourable half of the time, and due to that, the fish were sold for double the normal price. At first, the villagers would complain about it, but in the end they would accept it, for nothing could be done. On the other side of the kingdom, they managed to collect some crops from the fields, but in rainy winters it all went to waste, and they had to throw almost everything away. That is when the trading between kingdoms would start, sustaining each other until the bad weather ended.

And until Spring came.

And when it did, it wasn't just the trees that blossomed with new life.

2

One fine day in spring, a man with dark brown hair and a ducktail beard was pacing nervously in a big hall. His child was about to be born. Seff, one of the knights whose custom was to stay close to the king, watched this play out through his visor. Although he was known to be a serious soldier, the behaviour of the king, who was going to be a father for the first time, amused him.

Seff had short brown hair and a well-trimmed and extended goatee beard. He was the most fearless of all the knights, and he had a scar on the right side of his face which went from his eyebrow to the bottom of his chin. He was the oldest son in his family and had taken on many responsibilities at a young age, causing him to develop a solemn personality.

As well as carrying a sword, Seff liked to carry an axe, and he had no qualms about using it if he felt threatened. He had learnt many skills while taking care of his brothers and sisters. He had become an excellent hunter. Many times, he had gone off alone to find and gather food. Many times, he would return late in the night with his prey in his hands.

The news that the king was about to have his first child had spread like wildfire, and Seff knew that there were many villagers waiting outside the castle hoping to have a glimpse of the prince who would one day be their king.

Then, along the long corridors of the castle, he heard footsteps treading faster and faster.

The footsteps stopped in front of the hall door. After a quick knock, the door opened. It was a servant, and he was struggling to speak.

"My Lord!" The servant said between deep breaths. "Your..." he stopped for a moment. "Your child is born."

"Quick! Take me to him!" The king said, lifting his arms with excitement.

Seff escorted the king to the queen's bed chamber. Even as he approached, he could sense that many people in the room were in distress. Something wasn't right. When they entered, he heard a loud cry, the sign of a healthy child. The king was happy and walked towards the maidservant. The woman looked down while she handed the child over. The king removed the royal robe in which the baby was wrapped.

A frown appeared on his face. "It is... a girl!" The king stopped and stared at the baby's fragile body.

The room went quiet. The king had wanted a boy, everyone knew it. Some of the bystanders were fidgeting with their fingers. Then, without warning, the king started laughing. The people in the room looked relieved.

The king looked at his daughter with compassion, caressing her soft cheeks, holding her tiny and delicate hands in his.

"She is my little girl," he whispered. "Her name will be Rebekah." He lifted his gaze from his daughter's eyes and looked at the servants. "Remove this royal robe, for it does not suit a princess. Bring a pink one, quickly!"

The servants brought the robe to the king who dressed Rebekah in its bright folds. He held his daughter close to his chest and walked towards the balcony, where he lifted her high so that everybody could see.

When the villagers saw the pink robe, they fell silent. They were expecting a prince but seeing that the king himself was presenting her to them with beaming pride, they joined him in his joy and shouted with excitement, waving flags with the symbol of the kingdom emblazoned upon them.

The king announced that there would be a feast to celebrate and then went back to the room and ordered his councillor to distribute food and beer among the villagers outside. Ysabel, his wife, frowned at him. Knowing what she meant by the look in her eyes, he added, "Make sure that none of the food is wasted. And make sure that everyone receives one portion." When the villagers began to eat and drink, this was all accompanied by the sound of music and with exuberant dancing. The celebration was a success.

When everyone left after night fell, the king became curious to see what gifts his daughter had been given. He was amazed to see so many, but one of them caught his attention. It was a very familiar object - small, but with an important symbol printed on it.

How could this have got here? He thought.

The king opened the small box, finding a golden ring and medallion inside. The ring had three precious shiny sapphire stones, and the medallion had an even bigger one. It was pretty, and he couldn't deny his daughter deserved such a wonderful gift. But the king was puzzled. Only two people could have given such a lavish present, and they both lived far away.

The king sent a messenger to one of them, but due to the distance that separated them, it would be a while before she knew. Staffan knew nothing about the other one. He hadn't heard anything since he had become king.

I am sure it is him. But why now? he mused, rubbing his beard while staring at the stone.

The king walked to his daughter's room and approached her cot.

"Shhhh!" Ysabel whispered. "I've just got her to sleep, Staffan!"

The king placed the small box in a drawer and exchanged a quick smile with his wife before going out of the room.

In the following days, the king decided to organize his daughter's future education. Since he wanted the best for her, he asked his councillor, who without hesitation told him about a humble man who lived in the village by the sea. This man had travelled all over the world and learnt many things. His hair was as grey as his head was wise. When asked, he said he was honoured and delighted that the king had approached him, and he accepted the task.

When Staffan's sister came to visit the next day, he discovered that she hadn't given their mother's jewellery to his daughter, which only meant that it had been in the possession of his brother. Istha was his younger sister. After marrying Ruphus, a prince from a distant kingdom, she left Norandia to live with him, only visiting the family for important events. Her visit had been short, but just long enough to give them time to catch up.

The king was happy to have a daughter, but he still desired to have a son who would carry the family name.

Three years later, his dream came true.

One day, he was waiting in the great hall, when a servant came rushing in looking for him. "My lord! My lord! Your child is born!"

"Child?" The king lifted his eyebrow. "Can you be more specific?"

"Your..." the servant took another deep breath. "Your son!"

"A boy! Let us see him then!"

When the king arrived, escorted by Seff, his son was crying in the arms of the midwife. The king took his son. "He looks like me," he whispered. His lips didn't seem to move as he spoke. "His name will be Benjamen!"

He gave the boy a warm hug, then began to head towards the balcony.

On the way, he was brought to a halt by a maidservant. "My Lord!" she said. "The queen has not finished giving birth."

"What?" Staffan's eyes were fit to pop out of his head.

Ysabel was now shouting in pain. It seemed that her other son was comfortable in his mother's womb and didn't want to come out, but with an insistent final push, he at last emerged. The king was so happy that he started to laugh loudly.

The maidservant washed the second baby and gave him to the king, who took him and walked towards the balcony. The king showed off his two sons, and the crowd responded with an exuberant shout of joy. The first son was on his right arm and the second son on his left.

"Long live King Staffan and his sons!" The crowd cried.

On returning to the chamber, Staffan told everybody that he was going to call his second son Jakob. "When they are old enough," the king decreed, "my two sons will each be given a fortress."

There were four distant fortresses, positioned at the borders of the kingdom. The fortress north of the castle was going to be for the firstborn son, Benjamen. He would have the privilege of looking over the marvellous lake in the north-eastern side of the kingdom.

The fortress located east of the castle was going to be for his second son, Jakob. This had an ample view of great fields of barley and corn and its mission was to protect the barns which had been constructed to store the harvest.

There were another two fortresses, one south of the castle facing the green woods, the other to the west situated near to the coast, tasked with keeping watch over the ships that sailed the sea.

All four fortresses had a thick and tall stone wall linked to two of their sides that were close to ten thousand feet long each. At the end of each side, the wall took a forty-five-degree curve and carried on for another three thousand feet before it finished. Along the walls there were several small towers equipped with weapons designed to stop any invasion, and in front of the wall there was a slope which lead to deep ditches, which would help to slow down attackers in the event of an assault.

Four years later, Ysabel gave birth again to another boy, who was called Markus. Two years later, at sunrise, yet another boy joined the family, and he was named Luckas. He wasn't the last child, for two years later Ysabel gave birth to Shanna.

The king thought that it was a blessing from God to be able to have so many children. His wife, on the other hand, thought that it was just far too much for her. Fortunately, they had many maidservants who could help Ysabel with all her children.

These children were known everywhere in Norandia.

From Rebekah, being the oldest, through Benjamen, Jakob, Markus and Luckas, to Shanna who was the youngest.

3

For many years the king wasn't involved in any wars and so the people lived in peace. Even so, the king knew that no matter how good the times were, there would always be evil in the world, so he maintained the law which established that all young adults had to join his army. This law had been in force for many generations. However, since wars had become a distant memory, some parents had started to complain about it.

Within the kingdom there were twelve villages which were watched over by the four fortresses. Each fortress had three villages in their jurisdiction. Ruling over all was the king.

The king was interested to hear the concerns of his people, so once every three months he had a meeting with a spokesman from each village. He took time to hear all that they wanted to say, but as the king, he had the final vote and could choose what to do. Sometimes he would agree to the matter, and other times he would just ignore it.

The meetings took place in a sparse and spacious chamber in the castle. This room was illuminated by two big windows and several lampstands. A long and rectangular table stood in the middle of the room, and around it, were the chairs for each member of each village and the chairs for the king and his councillor. Whenever these meetings took place, two armed guards stayed on the outside of the door to avoid any disruption.

The day allocated for the meeting arrived, and the twelve men entered the room and sat on their appointed seats. As soon as the king entered with his councillor, the meeting started.

"My lord," The spokesman from one of the villages close to the great lake brought up the first issue. "The people are complaining, they think it is..." he moved his lips from side to side whilst trying to find a better word to use. "They think it is *unreasonable* to keep training the young boys and girls."

The king looked around the table before he replied. "I understand that parents want to be with their children and that they need their help," the king said, "but we need to be prepared for any invasion. I am aware, that there has been no threat of war, but that doesn't mean there won't be."

Everyone was quiet.

"On the other hand," the king continued. "We could reduce the number of years required. Are there any objections to that?"

Everyone shook their heads.

"My lord, I have another matter," a villager said.

"Go ahead."

"We understand that there have to be taxes, but why do the people who live by the sea have to pay more than the rest?"

The king looked at his councillor in surprise, for he knew nothing about that matter. "Well," the king said, keeping his calm, "this is news to me. I will see what I can do."

The king paused, then shouted for the guards.

When they entered, everyone could sense his rising anger.

"Bring me the tax collector in charge of the west side of the kingdom," the king barked.

An hour later, when the meeting was still in full flow, the soldiers returned empty-handed.

"My lord..." the soldier's sweat was pouring down his forehead. "There is no sign of the tax collector. His house is empty, and he was last seen yesterday afternoon."

The king stood up and walked towards the window. He stared through it at the forest. Then he smiled and spoke, turning to the people. "First of all, the tax for the villagers by the sea will be reset as the same as for everyone else in my kingdom. Then, we will need a new tax collector, after we have found the existing one."

"But where is he?" The spokesman from one of the villages by the sea was eager for justice. "The soldier says he has vanished."

The king turned to the soldiers. "I need you to find Seff and tell him to take five men and go south towards the woods. Maybe that's where he is hiding, before leaving the kingdom and fleeing to one of our neighbours."

"How can you be so sure, my lord?" asked another spokesman as the soldier marched quickly from the room.

"I will tell you," the king replied. "Imagine you have done something wrong and you want to move about without being seen. When is the best time to move without being noticed?"

"At night," the councillor replied.

"Exactly, and during the day he has to hide. Where is the best place?"

"The woods."

"Precisely."

Everyone was now smiling.

"Now if you'll excuse me," the king said. "We have been together long enough for today and I have some children who need my attention."

The king stood, as did everyone else in the room, and walked towards the door as his courtiers bowed. After he left, there was great appreciation for the king's wisdom. Only one of the spokesmen was silent. He had sunk into his own thoughts and started shivering.

"Everything fine my friend?" one of the men asked.

"Yes, I've just caught a bit of a cold." He said with a cough and a splutter.

As was the custom, the spokesmen returned after the meeting to their respective villages and rang the church bells three times. This alerted everyone that there was news to be shared at sunset, after the villagers had finished work. To make the place comfortable, there were seats positioned all around a wooden platform, from where the spokesman made his announcements.

The darkness was closing in, so there were lamps in every corner to give enough light for the people to see where they were stepping.

As the people went in, you could hear them murmuring.

"What's he going to say?" some asked.

"Better be good news," others muttered.

4

Seff was known for his outstanding hunting skills. He was persistent, never stopping until his assignment had been accomplished. In the case of the dishonest taxman, it only took him two days. Once in the woods, he had simply to follow the man's recent footprints and the broken branches above. At one point, Seff thought that he had lost his prey; the tracks he had been following led him in circles. It wasn't until he discovered a snapped twig that he found the man hiding behind a bush. The five soldiers who had followed Seff arrested the man and dragged him all the way to the castle.

The king, meanwhile, was attending to other important matters, and on this occasion, he had taken advantage of the sunshine and decided to speak with his generals in the courtyard. It wasn't too hot, and the air was fresh - a good combination - but the tranquil atmosphere didn't last long. Staffan was speechless when he saw Seff enter; he was amazed that his knight and soldiers had fulfilled another of his missions so effectively. There was the taxman, stubborn and uncooperative, before his eyes.

The tax collector stood before the king. His clothes were torn and dishevelled. His face and hands were grimy, his nails full of dirt. One of his eyes was purple and bruised.

"My lord!" Seff intoned. "As you suspected, this man was hiding in the woods."

"Well, well!" the king said. "So, you tried to steal and go unpunished. Where is the money?"

"My Lord," Seff said. "I'm afraid we found him empty-handed."

The king stood observing the man. He reasoned that Seff had already interrogated the suspect. He wasn't giving anything away, nor was he handing anything back.

"I think I know the perfect man for this," the king said.

"I can do it, my lord."

"I know you can, Seff, but by the look of his face you have bruised him enough, and he still does not want to speak. Take him to Ahron."

"Yes, my lord!"

Within an hour, Seff had found Ahron reading a book which Shemuel had given him. He had a big bedroom to himself. Nobody dared share a room with him because his pet puma was terrifying.

Ahron was an average-sized man with short, red hair and a well-cared for circular beard which made him look older than he was. He had a cluster of freckles on his cheeks which made him adorable to some of the women.

Ahron had been brought up by his uncle, after his parents had suffered a fatal and tragic accident. This uncle had taught him everything he knew about the natural world. He had many skills, and one of them was that he could touch any piece of soil and explain what had happened there. Then there were the puma and the eagle he kept as pets.

Seff knocked on the door and entered. "Ahron, the king wants you to make the tax collector talk."

Ahron nodded.

"Bring him in!"

Seff brought the tax collector into the room and thrust him into the seat of a chair.

"Talk," Ahron said.

The man was silent. He wasn't looking at Ahron. His attention was fixed on the puma next to his master. A bead of sweat dropped from the tax collector's forehead as the creature yawned, bearing its long, sharp incisors.

"It is not me who is going to persuade you to talk," Ahron said. "It is my puma. She is a clever cat. She also likes to toy with rodents. Rodents like you. Rodents that do not cooperate."

The puma's eyes seemed to glow in the dark chamber.

"I'm not going to fall for your tricks," the tax collector said. But the slight tremor in his voice betrayed his true feelings.

In the blink of an eye, the puma jumped, causing the man and his chair to fall to the ground. The man screamed.

"Where is the money?"

No answer.

"Where is it?"

Silence.

"One more time, where is the money?"

Nothing.

"Sasha. Finish him!"

The puma placed one of her paws on the tax collector's chest. As she started to knead the man, his breathing became more erratic. The great cat seemed to smile as she leaned down and breathed on his face. As the cat's claws started to pierce his skin, blood-red stains began to appear on his grubby shirt. There was now no escape. The man was trapped.

"I don't believe you!" he yelled.

"You don't believe what?" Ahron said.

"That you'll allow this thing to eat me!"

"You have little faith, then."

Ahron snapped his fingers and the puma lunged forward, taking one of the man's earlobes in her teeth, her saliva dripping down his neck, cold and wet. The man was shaking now.

"Alright! Alright!" he yelped. "I'll talk."

"Sasha, stay," Ahron said.

"It was the spokesman from the first village by the sea," the prisoner panted. He said that he would keep it until things calmed down, then I would return, then he would give me my share!"

Ahron snapped his fingers three times. The cat roared, its growl deep and resonant, coming from the very pit of her belly.

"I'm telling the truth!" the man insisted.

Ahron waited for a moment, then told Sasha to withdraw.

Sasha licked the man's face from chin to forehead and stepped backwards nonchalantly, heading back to her mattress. Ahron threw her a bloody slice of meat which she tore apart as if it was paper.

Ahron repeated what the tax collector had said to three guards who were outside his door. Two of them carried the man by his arms to a cell, while the third went with Seff to inform the king.

Staffan couldn't believe it when he heard the news. He had trusted these officials and allowed them to do their jobs without any controls. Now, thanks to two greedy men, everything would have to change.

"Bring all the spokesmen and tax collectors to me," he snapped.

Messengers were dismissed straightaway to all parts of the kingdom. It was night, but the king was so angry he didn't care. He wanted to solve the matter straight away. The men would have to obey the king's command. They would have to travel to the castle without delay.

Seff was in the group that headed for the treacherous spokesman. When the culprit had been arrested, Seff and his soldiers lit their torches and entered the man's house. His wife tried to stop them as they moved the furniture, complaining that she would have to put everything back in place after they had gone. When she realised all her moaning was to no avail, she started crying in despair. Not even the inquisitive villagers could help her, for the soldiers outside the door were denying them entrance.

"What are you looking for?" demanded the woman once she composed herself.

"None of your business!" Seff removed a wooden cabinet from the wall as he spoke.

"Why are you making such a mess?"

"Your husband has something which does not belong to him," Seff answered.

"He has nothing!"

"Sir!" one of the soldiers said. He had been using the end of a stick to prod around the floorboards. "Under this carpet, there is a hollow sound."

The soldiers removed the carpet.

"Asha!" Seff said.

There, beneath his feet, was a small wooden door. He opened it to find some stairs which descended into what resembled a cellar. Once inside, and with the help of their torches, Seff and the soldiers found the money stashed in wooden fishing crates.

"I didn't even know that was there!" the woman shouted as they ascended the steps and stood before her.

Seff stared at the woman who was now uttering an unbroken string of unrepeatable profanities, calling her husband every disgusting name under the sun as the soldiers brought up the boxes full of the king's money.

"Leave her," Seff said to the soldiers as they departed.

Seff and his men mounted their horses and before long joined the main column heading back to the castle. All the tax collectors and spokesmen were grumpy. They had been escorted from their homes and forced to ride to the castle many miles away. The men were cold and confused, demanding that Seff explain what was happening. But Seff said nothing.

When they arrived at the castle gate, they were led into a damp and empty chamber, lit only by a few guttering candles above.

"You will be wondering why I have summoned you with such urgency."

The men recognised the voice. They knelt. To the king.

"Some time ago, somebody raised taxes in my kingdom without my knowledge and thought that his actions would go unnoticed, that he would become rich without me finding out."

There were gasps in the room.

"Here is the man!"

The king emerged from the shadows and turned towards the doors. They were opened slowly. A terrified man entered the chamber, his teeth chattering, his clothes dotted with blood and mud.

"This man stole money that was owed to the crown," the king said. "But the matter does not end there. One of you has also betrayed me."

The gasps were louder now.

The king lifted his arm and the room fell silent again. He pointed at one of the men, portly and bald, cowering at the front.

"You," he said.

"No!" the man cried. "I would never steal from you, my lord!"

Just then, the soldiers who had searched the man's house marched in, bearing the crates of cash from his secret cellar.

Seeing the haul, the man broke, begging for mercy.

All his colleagues looked at him appalled and shocked. They knew that they would never see him again.

"You know that theft does not go unpunished in my kingdom," the king said in a solemn voice. "And because you have also tried to lie to me, you will be sent to the cage."

"No!" the man screamed. "He forced me!"

"Who did?"

The condemned man raised his trembling arm and pointed a fat finger towards the tax collector. "It was his fault! I only obeyed orders!"

"Liar!" the tax collector shouted. "You were the one who forced me! You said we would never be caught!"

"Who forced you?" asked the king again.

"He did!" This time both men shouted in unison.

"Who?" The king had run out of patience.

But they wouldn't tell. They seemed to be resigned to their fate now.

"Take them to the cage at sunrise!" the king said to Seff. "I will be merciful to your families" the king continued, turning back to the prisoners. "Your wives and sons will not be punished for your crime."

Everyone knew about the cage. If you were able to escape from it alive, you would be set free of any charges, but nobody had ever done it. The cage was a large wooden box, twenty-seven feet long, thirteen feet wide and ten feet high. It was situated in a small valley in the south-west side of the kingdom, close to some tall, wide trees. The cage was divided into two sections by a sliding wooden wall, of which the smallest section was ten feet long. The only source of light was from the cracks and holes in the roof, and there wasn't enough light to be able to see. To enter, the person who was going to be punished had to go up some ladders that led to the roof. There a soldier would push him through a small door that was above the smaller section. Once in the interior, the sliding wall would be moved, revealing eight ferocious and hungry wolves. These wolves had to be taken care of and were usually fed every two days. Five of the king's soldiers camped at a safe distance to tend and feed them.

At sunrise, Seff brought the men to their place of execution. Both pleaded for mercy, but it was too late for them. He pushed both men through the hole using the tip of his blade. There was the sound of scurrying and tears in the darkness.

Then the sliding door started to move.

The men were whimpering now.

There was the sound of a howl, a primal yell from the depths of the first wolf. Then a second howl. Then a third.

They were hunting.

Sniffing.

Picking up the men's scent.

Then there was an enraged growl, more growls, and the sound of screams. And tearing, ripping noises.

Then, after a few more groans, silence.

The spokesmen and tax collectors who had been forced to come to the castle from their homes looked on horrified.

"Tell everyone what you have seen," the king declared. "Let this be a lesson for all. Anyone who steals from the king will suffer the same fate as these two men. There will be no mercy."

Seff looked at the frightened and pale faces. He knew that they would think twice before ever crossing their king again.

Norandia

5

The following day, as the king was walking beside the lake thinking over his affairs, he tried to remember what the tax collector and the spokesman had said. They were both in agreement on one thing, and that was that they had been forced. *Did one force the other? Or was there someone else involved?* His mind was a whirlpool of questions.

While immersed in his thoughts, the king didn't see the soldier galloping towards him.

"My lord! My lord!" shouted the soldier.

"What is it?" replied the king, snapping out of his thoughts.

"You are wanted in the castle. A messenger has arrived with news."

"Take me to him, fast!"

The king mounted his horse and the two rode to the castle where the tired messenger was being revitalised with fresh water and food. He had travelled a long distance to see Staffan. When the king entered, the messenger, weary though he was, rose to his feet, wiped his mouth with a serviette and bowed.

"My lord," said the messenger when he had raised his head. "I have news from your brother Kidron."

"Speak!"

"Your brother wants to see you."

"Could he not have come himself?"

"No sir, not after you…"

The king waved the rest of the statement away before it had even left the man's lips. "All right! Tell him I will see him in twelve days at the tree where we used to camp when we were younger. Does that leave you enough time?"

"Yes sir."

"If that is all, you can go. However, if you need to stay one day so that you and your horse can rest, I have no objection to that."

"Thank you, my lord, but the journey is long. I should depart as soon as possible."

"In that case, the cook will give you some food for the journey."

The king turned to leave the room. It was getting late and the candles were mere stumps now, so he headed to his chambers, where his footman lit a fire and helped him out of his royal uniform.

That night, the king couldn't sleep so he decided to breathe in a bit of fresh air, hoping that it would help him. He went to the balcony and looked out across his kingdom. The only source of light was the moon and a few torches belonging to the night watchmen moving on the walls.

"Why now?" His thoughts were carried like a whisper on the breeze. "Why does he want to come and see me, after so many years?"

That moment, he heard the noise of rustling silk behind him, the soft and familiar tread of ornate slippers on the stone floor. The rose scent was confirmation. The king did not need to turn around.

"Is there anything troubling you, my dear?" said Ysabel, placing her arm in his. "I heard you mumbling."

"Nightmare," the king muttered, not wanting to alarm his wife.

"Come back to bed," she said, her voice soothing and soft. "There is nothing to fear."

The king turned and smiled, hoping the sense of trouble would not surface in his weary eyes.

"There is nothing to fear," his wife said, as she led him back to bed.

But the king was not convinced.

Not convinced at all.

Norandia

6

Before the king could depart on his journey to meet his brother, he had to attend to matters of state business, and whatever spare time he had he spent it with his children. During the day he had a very tight schedule with not much time to think, but when the night arrived everything changed. All he could do was worry about what might take place when he saw his brother.

One night before his journey, a night with a full moon, the king was wide awake and having difficulty sleeping. He knew all too well that his brother was a better fighter. If swords were drawn, he would almost certainly lose. *What am I thinking? He is my brother, he won't do me any harm, will he?*

Unable to sleep, the king slipped outside for a walk. As he left the entrance to his chambers, he noticed that the guards weren't standing at his door. *Where have they gone?* He thought.

The king walked down the long stone staircase and down a long passageway until he reached the courtyard.

No one seemed to be awake.

Everything was silent.

Everyone had disappeared.

Suddenly, he heard a gruff voice in the darkness. "Staffan!"

"Who is speaking?" The king asked. "I will shout for the guards!"

"You have nothing to fear."

"Show yourself then!"

The voice didn't reply.

Silence.

The king wasn't carrying a torch so he couldn't see who it was, even under the shimmering light of the silvery moon. He reached out into the shadows, but there was nothing. No one.

Then, without warning, he heard a thump at his feet. Someone had thrown something.

The king knelt and drew both hands around the object. It felt like a long stick wrapped in some sort of textile material. The king grabbed it just as the mysterious man spoke again.

"Fight!" he said.

As he spoke, several torches were lit, but again, there was not enough light for the king to see who was addressing him.

It had been a while since the king had duelled with someone, and even though he was out of practice, he wasn't going to allow a stranger to intimidate him. As he focused on the shadows, he saw the form of the unknown man heading towards him. The king raised the stick to defend himself. But he was out of practice, for the attacker's blows rained down time and again, causing the stick to fall from his hands.

"Pick it up," said the man.

The king stooped and grasped the pole. He thrust at his opponent, but each of his lurches was repelled.

As time went by, the king began to feel the strength ebbing from his body. If he didn't do something soon, he would have to surrender. He didn't want to do that. He didn't even know who it was he was fighting.

The king stepped back to take a breath, resting for a second from the blows he was giving and receiving.

"Where are my guards?" the king asked, playing for more time.

"What have you done with them?"

This had troubled him since he had left his chambers. The knights were sworn to protect him even at the cost of their own lives, and most certainly to the end of them. He couldn't work out why they weren't rushing to his aid, not least because of the sound of the blows.

The only answer the king received was a blow to his side.

The fight continued until the first bright splashes of colour and light appeared on the horizon. It was time for one more move. The king put all his energy and focus into one precise strike that caused his opponent's weapon to fly out of his hands. Seeing this, the king leapt forward and threw his arms around the man, trying to pin him down. But the man was too strong and too clever. He drew a sharp object from his left thigh and poked him with it, causing the king to wince at the bolt of pain.

"Tell me your name!" the king said, stumbling backwards.

The man stepped back, his head and face still shrouded by the darkness, and by what looked to the king like a monk's cowl. "I am a friend not a foe," he said, "And you are now ready to meet your brother. If he should challenge you, you will give a good account of yourself."

With that, he turned and leaped over the battlements, climbed down the tree as nimbly as a cat, and disappeared into the last vestiges of the night.

As the light grew brighter, two sentries came running to the king, who was now kneeling, holding his side, staunching the flow of blood from the wound he had just suffered.

"My lord! Is everything all right?" one of them asked.

The king was not in a mood to be comforted. "Did you not see him? Are you blind? Follow him and arrest him? Now!"

"Who, my lord?" the other sentry asked, his knees trembling.

"My assailant, you fool."

"But we didn't see anyone," the first sentry said.

"Sir! You are bleeding!" the other man said, staring at the red stain on his king's nightshirt.

The king let them help him to his quarters where he was visited by a doctor who sewed up the knife wound having administered a potion which he claimed would mask the pain.

It didn't.

The king was now more concerned than ever, and he ordered his guards to redouble their numbers and their efforts, especially during the watches of the night.

7

The morning of the departure dawned, and the king rose from his bed, his body sore from the blows, but resolved to be at peace about the meeting with his brother. He had given a good account of himself in the mysterious duel he had encountered. And besides, what did he have to fear? He would have seven of his best knights with him, and Ahron's puma.

"It will be good to see your brother after so long," remarked Ysabel, as she sat with Staffan at breakfast.

"It will."

"One thing strikes me as strange," Ysabel said.

"What's that, my love?"

"Why does he need to meet you so far away?"

"It was I who arranged the location. Don't you remember what happened last time he was here?"

"He was very discourteous that day," Ysabel said, looking into the far distance.

"But that's not what strikes me as strange," the king said. "It's more the time than the place."

"What do you mean, husband?"

"I mean, why now? Why this precise moment, after so long?"

"Well, I am sure there's a perfectly sound and harmless explanation," she said. "He is your brother, after all."

"I hope you are right," the king said with a sigh.

At midday, all the preparations for the journey had been completed, and the king and seven of his knights were mounted, ready to depart. In order to lighten their load, the horses were burdened only with essential equipment and provisions, such as sacks of food, bits of bedding. Before the king said his final farewell, he ordered his generals to be on high alert for any invading forces.

"All this could be a decoy," he said. "Keep careful watch while I'm away. The safety of Norandia is in your hands."

As the small band headed out of the castle courtyard, people waved and cheered the travellers on their way. Then, in the hours that followed, the king and his knights crossed several shallow rivers where they gathered the freshest water into their leather-skinned canteens. As the men filled their bags, they watched in the crystal-clear water as shoals of silver fish struggled upstream against the current, heading towards a small waterfall where they would leap from the foamy waves. As evening was now approaching, several of the men took rods from the flanks of their steeds and threw lines out, with bread wedged tightly around tiny hooks. It took all their skill to catch anything, but in the end, four fish lay on the bank of the river, their tailfins flapping, their eyes gawping wide.

"Not quite enough for dinner!" The king cried as the fishermen among them gutted their haul, leaving the innards for the birds that were even now beginning to hover and dart above.

While two of the knights went off foraging for kindling, another two prepared their arrows, straightening their feathers and making their bows as tight as the fishermen's. When they were ready, they stood still in the river, their bows poised above the sparkling water, ready to shoot an arrow.

In the hour that followed, there was much splashing and no little laughter as the knights missed nine times out of ten. However, the one time out of ten that they did strike, made all the effort worthwhile. Now there was a further catch of six fish, enough to feed the whole group. As the fish guts were removed, the foragers returned carrying bundles of wood and a fire was lit. Each man was given a hunk of bread and a long stick on which they cooked their own meat. When the flesh of the fish was sizzling, the oil causing the fire to roar and spit, they made a sandwich and filled their bellies, washing the food down with gulps of the pure water from the river.

As the sun went down, the many shades of green in the bushes, grass banks and lowering trees disappeared into the darkness. When the only source of light was the dying fire and the moon, the men unrolled their bedding and lay down. Even the king, who was used to sleeping in far greater luxury, slept on a carpet. All the knights shared in the king's watch. Two knights stayed awake at each side of him throughout the night, while the puma purred at the king's feet.

"Seff," the king said, to the loyal knight next to him. The other night, it was you wasn't it? In the cowl, with the stick, duelling with your king."

Seff was silent.

"Thank you," the king said.

There was still no answer.

The king smiled.

The two men fell silent.

In this open ground, nothing could be heard except for the whispering of the wind, revealing its innermost secrets to anyone who would care to listen. Thousands of stars spread over the thick black sky. As the king studied them, he remembered how as a boy he would join them like dots, forming the lines into figures and shapes in his mind's eye. Before he fell asleep, he saw a shooting star dashing like lightning across the sky, leaving a trace of unimaginable colours behind. As he closed his eyes, the king smiled.

The next day, they rose and washed before mounting their

horses and heading off through a green and lush meadow, where the tall grass concealed an abundance of wildlife, undisturbed until their arrival. As the horses nickered and neighed, the concealed animals scurried away in all directions. From the meadows, the band moved to rocky and dry ground where, in the past, two rivers had given life to all the vegetation nearby, but when they dried up, all that was around them withered away, leaving a barren space.

Finally, after leaving this rocky terrain, they rode along the mountainside and then began the journey uphill, moving ever closer to their destination and the meeting with the king's brother. This meeting, however, was not uppermost in the king's mind. He had forgotten how beautiful the landscape was outside his castle. He had stayed too long within its walls. Now, he was so lost in wonder at the rich diversity of the natural habitats of Norandia that the impending encounter had momentarily slipped out of his focus. As they reached the summit, they followed a dirt path which led them to the tree. The path had clearly been used by recent travellers, as the bushes and branches on both of its sides were not intruding at all. From this path, it was impossible not to see the tree as it was the tallest there, affording generous shade with its thick crown of green leaves.

The king told four of his knights, including Ahron and his puma, to keep watch as he and his escort headed towards the tree. "I used to camp at the tree with my brother when we were boys," the king said to Seff who was riding just behind him. "We used to climb here often. It was our favourite place, both of us, away from the castle."

"It offers a great view," Seff said. The king nodded as the two men looked down into the green valleys stretching as far as their eyes could see.

As the king approached the tree he could see how its roots had begun to burst from the surface in their determination to expand. But this was not all he noticed. Standing beside the vast trunk of the tree was his brother. The king could tell that he was impatient.

"My brother!" the man bellowed. "You are looking well!"

"I can say the same of you," the king said as he dismounted.

"You have come with three of your knights," his brother said chuckling. "I see you still don't trust me!"

"Don't take it personally. There are certain, shall we say, protocols…"

"But I'm your brother. What harm can come to you?"

The king frowned.

"Look," his brother said, spotting his sceptical look. "I'm sorry for what happened last time. How many more times will I have to say it?"

The king dismissed Seff, Kristal and Yosef who kept within range, allowing just enough distance so that the two brothers could have some privacy. Seff and Yosef kept their eyes on the king while Kristal inspected the surroundings. Kristal was born and blessed with sharp eyesight and an acute sense of hearing. As her wavy brown hair twitched in the wind, her blue eyes scanned the area for any hint of an ambush. The king looked back at her for a moment, smiling as he watched her sniffing the air like a deer. She was serious, deadly serious, and yet mysterious too. She had lost her parents at a very young age and been brought up by her uncle and aunt. She had received a good education in a humble home. She had studied hard and done well, but every night she had gone to bed with the same thought, that one day she would avenge her parents. When she became a knight, she turned out to have great skill with the sword, but whenever she used an axe she became lethal. It was almost as if every blow she struck was to the throats of those who had killed her father and her mother.

As the king turned back to his brother, he resumed the conversation. "I have not travelled this long journey to argue, brother. What do you want?"

"I want half of your kingdom."

"You're joking."

"I'm deadly serious."

"What grounds have you for making such a preposterous demand."

"Your kingdom has been growing. So has your family. All this is far too much for one man. Let your beloved brother give you a helping hand. To ease the load, give you more time with all your children." Kidron grinned, but the king knew that it was a fake smile.

"You know my answer," the king said.

Kidron stopped smiling.

"Our father made it very clear before he died," the king said. "He told us both that you are very irresponsible. That's why he gave me the kingdom, and you the lands beyond Norandia."

"That was more of a curse than a blessing," Kidron said.

"It was fertile land when our father gave it to you," the king replied. "What have you …?"

"My servants have ruined it," Kidron interrupted with a scowl.

"It's not the servants but you who rules the land," the king said, his voice firm, his tone grave.

"You sound just like Father," Kidron said. Then he seemed to snap himself out of his melancholy and a smile began to stretch across his face. "Did Rebekah like her jewellery?"

"What?" the king was shocked. "How did you know she was born?"

"I cannot reveal all my secrets, brother."

"Did you steal it from our mother?"

Before the king could answer, Krystal was by his side. She had been looking up into the blue sky and noticed Ahron's eagle flying in circles overhead. This had been the signal agreed before they had left the other knights. They had been ordered to send this signal at any sign of trouble.

"My lord, we should be going."

"Are you expecting anybody?" the king asked.

"Why do you want to know, brother?"

"You have not changed," the king said.

"But we have only just started our discussions."

"There's nothing more to discuss," the king said, his voice marked by a growing note of anger. "There will be no division to my kingdom. You, brother, will remain as ruler of the far country. I bid you farewell." The king walked to his horse and leaped into the saddle.

Kidron was quiet.

But his eyes were on fire.

As the king returned to his four remaining knights, he could see that they had been in a fight. Several had flesh wounds to their face. One was receiving treatment from the knight who, as second string to his bow, had trained as a doctor. Ahron's puma was licking the blood from its master's hand.

"What happened?" the king asked.

"Your brother was planning an ambush, my lord," Tytus said between breaths. "We saw a glint of armour in the trees. We got to them just in time. Gave them a good beating, we did."

Tytus had short blond hair and brown eyes. He was known as "the honourable knight". He had vast knowledge, a poet's love of language and unusual powers of persuasion. He was a good fighter; something that ran in his blood. His father had excelled at it too. He wasn't just a master swordsman; he was a fine archer as well.

"If you think we look rough," Tytus said, "you should see them, sire!"

A laugh erupted from the depths of the king's belly.

"Good work!" he shouted. "That'll make my brother mad! He'll almost certainly kill the officer in charge of the men who attacked you. He can't control himself when things go wrong!"

The king stared at his four warriors with a look of undisguised pride. Tytus, Tabitha, Feliks and Ahron had been tested in the fire that morning and they had showed their mettle. So had Ahron's puma, and his eagle.

When their wounds had been dressed, they broke camp and mounted their horses. The eight of them in the troop, along with the big cat and the sharp-eyed bird of prey, headed back down the mountain before choosing a different route to the castle, one through shallow rivers, leaving no tracks that Kidron and his men could follow. When the rivers led to a great lake, there the horses slaked their thirst and the knights filled their leather-skinned water carriers.

As the sun hid behind the mountains late in the day, darkness enveloped the land. The king and his knights resolved to continue their journey by the light of the moon, not resting until they had returned to the castle.

As the king's horse finished drinking, Tytus approached. "My lord, may I ask you a question?"

The king nodded.

"Your brother, do you think he will try to trick you again?"

"He won't stop until he has succeeded in his ambitions," the king said. "That's one thing I do still know about him. He's persistent. We should be ready for the worst."

Tytus was about to leave when the king added, "One more thing. When we were on much higher ground, overlooking this lake, I remember seeing two castles not far from here. I would like to visit them on our way home. If the war clouds are gathering, maybe it's time to form some new alliances."

"Very well, sire," Tytus said. "I'll give the order."

8

Six years passed and there was no word from the king's brother. While the people lived in peace, the king was far from relaxed. He expected his brother to act anytime. For him, the sense of tranquillity in his kingdom was nothing more than an illusion. The grey flecks of hair on his head were ample proof of the lack of serenity in his troubled soul.

All the while, the king's children were growing fast, and he knew that sometime in the future he would have to put some of them in charge of the fortresses. By doing so, he would be able to observe their ability to rule over a small number of people and an allocated piece of land. In the meantime, they were all taught in the same classroom - a small room with big windows through which the sun's rays passed. As they sat in line, from youngest to oldest, the teacher would stand in front of them and explain the different subjects that he had prepared for the day. On a typical day the children finished around lunchtime. After that, the boys were taken to a courtyard where they were given instruction on how to use a sword, using wooden replicas.

Among these children, Markus stood out with his two strong arms and muscular frame. Even though he was younger than his two twin brothers, he would always manage to beat them and ridicule them in front of the spectators. He was a natural fighter.

"Haha!" said Markus, aiming the tip of his wooden sword at the throat of his fallen brother. "I win again Benjamen!"

Benjamen was furious. "One day I will be victorious!" He shouted, slamming the ground with his fist.

With this contest over, the eyes of the spectators turned to another duel.

"Look!" One of them cried. "Luckas is managing to hold on."

"Yes, but not for long," another said.

Luckas wasn't as strong as his brothers, but he had determination, and he always showed a lot of courage when he was fighting. Even if he fell to the ground, he would stand up as fast as he could and launch a counterattack.

"Do you give up?" Jakob asked him.

"Not yet!"

As soon as Luckas was on his feet again, he ran towards Jakob, aiming his sword at his brother's chest. Jakob, taking pity on his brother, ended the fight with a simple twist of the sword, sending Luckas' into the air.

"Well done, everybody!" shouted the knight training them. "You are all learning fast. We have finished for today. Return to your father."

As for the king's daughters, Rebekah went to spend some time with her mother, and Shanna wandered wherever she wanted. Shanna admired her older brothers and liked to play with them, but when her brothers were practising with their swords, she wasn't allowed to be with them. That was of no concern for her, for she found a spot behind a wooden wall where she couldn't be seen and could learn their moves from a safe distance. Practising with a small stick which she found on the ground wasn't much fun, so with some of her savings she went to a carpenter and she ordered her own wooden sword.

One day, while Rebekah was walking past the spot where Shanna spied on her brothers, she thought that she had seen through the corner of her eye her sister playing with a sword. Puzzled, she stopped and stepped backward to check if her suspicions were true.

It was indeed her sister, waving a sword with a great deal of vigour but very little skill.

"Shanna! What are you doing?"

Shanna froze for a few seconds before hiding the sword behind her back. "Nothing."

"Nothing?" Rebekah asked stepping forward.

"Nothing."

"So, what is that behind your back? Lift your right arm."

Shanna had no way out, but she tried to fool her sister by lifting her right arm, having left the sword in her other hand.

"Very clever! Now the left one."

"I… can… explain…" Shanna was stuttering as she raised her wooden sword.

"Where did you get that?"

"I cannot tell you."

"You know, my little sister, stealing is not right. That is what father has taught us."

"I did not steal it!"

"Just tell me where you got it, and I will not tell father."

Shanna thought for a moment, then gave in. "I bought it from a carpenter in the village, but I cannot tell you who. I promised him."

"Very well. But let me remind you what you are and are not allowed to learn. Come with me."

Rebekah took Shanna's hand and led her to her room, where she fetched a big brown bag from under her bed containing a bow and some arrows. "Don't ask any questions," she said. "We're heading out."

Once Rebekah had what she was looking for she searched for

Tabitha, the knight in charge of the princesses, and told her about her intentions, for they were still too young to go out of the castle alone. Tabitha was small, but that didn't bother her; she was as agile as a gazelle. What made her stand out from the other knights was her long red hair which she used to tie at the back when she wasn't wearing her helmet. Her father was a formidable hunter, and though her mother wasn't in agreement, Tabitha spent most of her young years learning from him many useful skills, such as how to use a bow and arrow.

Without delay, Tabitha searched for another knight called Feliks. Feliks was a tall young man with grey eyes and black hair who would take on any kind of challenge with a smile that reassured those around him. He was the youngest of them all and still had to learn a few skills, but he was determined to always give his best, and that was what made him adaptable to all circumstances.

Tabitha, the smallest of the knights, and Feliks, the youngest, went to prepare the horses. As soon as the girls arrived, they began their journey.

Shanna's excitement was increasing by the second, but at the same time she was rather suspicious, for they hadn't told her anything yet. They headed south, passing along the fortress and heading towards the woods. Once they were out of sight among the trees, one of the knights helped both girls to dismount.

"This is a secret location," Tabitha said.

Shanna looked around for clues, but as she had been told nothing, she didn't know what to look for, and her thoughts were starting to betray her.

What was so exciting about the woods?

Why keep all this a mystery?

"Father told me we could do this here..." Rebekah said.

"What? Do what?!"

"You will see, you just have to be patient. In fact, you're going to need a lot of patience, sister!"

As Shanna looked around, she saw that they were in a small open space surrounded by thick trees. The air was fresh, the grass was lit by sunbeams. Outside this illuminated spot, the air was damp and cold; very few of the sun's rays had made it through the many, leaf-laden branches. Inside, it was quiet and peaceful, undisturbed by the wind.

As the two knights took up their positions, Tabitha took off her helmet, revealing thick red hair that cascaded over her shoulders.

"She's pretty," said Shanna.

"Thank you," said the knight. "I'm going to show you how to shoot an arrow."

"Shoot what?" Shanna's eyes were popping with curiosity.

"You will see!"

Rebekah grabbed her bag with her bow and arrow.

"Wow!" Shanna's mouth was open in amazement.

One of the knights marched to the other end of the well-lit spot, grabbed a target from behind a tree and moved it forward so that they could start shooting their arrows. Shanna was the first. The knights wanted to see how she would manage on her own, without their instructions. She was enthusiastic and, after several attempts, she discovered that the back of the arrow had to go with the string of the bow. At all times, Tabitha was next to the princess watching to make sure that she didn't harm herself.

When she was ready, Shanna released her arrow. It travelled a small distance before going straight into the ground.

"You are still young," Rebekah laughed, shooting an arrow that found the target. "But with practice you will do well."

While Rebekah continued to shoot arrows, Tabitha took some

time to train Shanna. Even though Shanna was young, she was determined to become an expert archer. So, as time went on, Shanna often went to the woods with Tabitha and Feliks to continue with her training.

Rebekah only joined them from time to time.

And, as time went on, Shanna improved more and more.

Shanna's progress in the secret location was startling. On one occasion, she felt so relaxed and confident that when she let go of the string the arrow hit the very centre of the target. She was overjoyed.

"Well done Shanna!" Tabitha clapped.

Shanna was radiant. She had succeeded at last.

"Know this, my little princess." Tabitha leaned towards Shanna. "We never stop learning."

Tabitha grabbed two arrows and set them both in her bow.

"I'm going to teach you a new trick."

She stood still and aimed at the target whilst Feliks tried to distract her by clapping his hands and shouting. He didn't put her off; she was concentrating too hard, not allowing the noise to distract her. When ready, Tabitha smiled and then released both arrows. They travelled at full speed through the open space until they hit the target in the centre, next to Shanna's arrow.

"That's amazing!" Shanna shouted.

Shanna was impressed and determined to copy her tutor. She tried to remember all that Tabitha had done, but things didn't turn out well, both arrows tumbling to the ground. When she realized that she couldn't do it without counsel, Shanna turned to Tabitha. "Teach me how to do that," she said.

"With pleasure."

Shanna spent the rest of the morning practicing until it was nearly time for lunch. As the three of them finished archery, Shanna walked towards the knights with her hands behind her back and stopped right in front of Tabitha, whilst shuffling her feet from side to side.

"Tabitha, do you think you could show me how to fight with a sword?"

Feliks shot a surprised look at Tabitha, who then looked at Shanna. "Is that what you want, my princess?" asked Tabitha.

"Yes, I do."

"Will you keep it a secret? I do not think your father would approve."

"I will."

"Then we will need a wooden sword," Feliks said. "This one is too heavy and too sharp." He was pointing at his own sword.

Shanna ran towards the horse grazing by the trees and grabbed her brown bag. After shaking it several times, the wooden sword dropped to the ground.

"Where did you get that?" asked Feliks, clearly impressed.

"It's a secret," Shanna replied.

"Very well," Feliks said. "Let's get practicing."

One warm afternoon, Shanna and Rebekah went as usual to the woods to practise with Tabitha and Feliks. Yosef now started to join the group. He was a black muscular man with a shaved head. He used to be a slave, separated from his family at a young age, but he won his liberty by saving one of the king's generals when they were being attacked by looters at one of their camps. Even though he hadn't been treated well in his years of slavery, it didn't stop him from being a very amicable man.

After several hours of practising and enjoying the moment, the horses became restless, moving backwards and forwards, agitated at the presence of something or someone nearby. The knights shared a quick glance at each other and decided to leave and fast.

"It is time to go, girls!" Feliks steered them towards the horses.

"Why?" Shanna asked, her eyes filled with disappointment.

Feliks bent down and whispered into her ear. "We have visitors."

Tabitha took an arrow and aimed it towards the trees. Whatever it was, she had to be prepared. She looked around and tried to find a target, but the only thing she saw was the branches moving. Her father had always taught her that she had to be patient when hunting, and this was no exception.

Eventually, Tabitha decided it was the moment to act. "Come out!" she said. "I am ready!"

Yosef withdrew his sword and gazed into the trees but saw nothing. Whatever it was, it knew how to hide. In the meantime, Rebekah and Shanna jumped onto the same horse. Feliks mounted his own steed.

Just then, a group of soldiers appeared from behind the trees. They were screaming with fury. There were too many to fight.

Yosef stood behind Shanna and Rebekah on one horse, Feliks on the other. He was forming a rear guard.

"Run Feliks!" shouted Yosef.

Shanna was terrified.

The two horses galloped at full speed, avoiding all the trees in their way. As they continued towards the end of the woods, they found themselves confronted by some soldiers blocking their exit, forcing them to find another route. As Feliks tried to search for a quick way out, someone knocked him off his horse. He fell backwards and tried to recover, but two men grabbed him and dragged him away from the spot.

Now Rebekah on her own, manoeuvring the horse while

Shanna managed to overcome her fear and grabbed her bow and arrow. She aimed at one of the men dragging Feliks through the undergrowth.

If only my horse wasn't moving as much.

She concentrated on her targets, letting go of one arrow after another. Both soldiers were struck, one in the head, the other in the neck. Both fell down dead, one after the other.

Shanna had no time to congratulate herself. Rebekah was now screaming as two soldiers started pulling her down off her horse.

"Rebekah!"

"Help!"

Shanna remembered what she had been given some time ago for cases like this. It was a silver trumpet that had an unusual sound. When people heard it, they knew that one of the king's children was in trouble and the king's knights and soldiers would rush to their aid.

Without hesitation, Shanna took the trumpet from her bag and blew it with all her might, making birds in the surrounding trees fly in all directions.

No sooner had she given a long blast than one of the soldiers grabbed her and pulled her from the horse.

Tabitha and Yosef heard the trumpet, but there was little they could do; they were still fighting the soldiers who had rushed them in the clearing. Tabitha had been prudent in choosing her targets, but she soon ended up with no arrows, so she was forced to grab her sword to defend herself.

Behind her, Yosef was repelling the attacks against him. He was now standing back-to-back with Tabitha.

Feliks now grabbed his sword. He ran between the soldiers and, with lightning speed, thrust a sword into one man and a dagger into the other. He then turned on the soldier who had Shanna in his grip. Within a few heartbeats he had driven his blade into the soldier's heart.

"Where is Rebekah?" he asked.

For a moment he thought that he had lost her, but a scream made him think otherwise. He grabbed Shanna and ran towards the source of the noise.

"Quick!" he shouted. "Climb up this tree. I will try to rescue your sister."

Tabitha and Yosef were surrounded and had been forced to yield their swords. Feliks, seeing them, ran towards the soldiers. While he was moving forward with his sword raised, he saw some of them falling on their knees. As they then fell to the ground, he noticed arrows in their backs.

In a flash, there were eight knights on horseback in the middle of the chaos. They dismounted and raised their swords to fight.

The first knight to jump from her horse was Kristal. Her mission was to search for Rebekah and protect her whilst the other knights fought against the soldiers. Following her footsteps was Jaylon, who ran close to Kristal to cover her back. Jaylon was a tall man with cropped blond hair. His favourite weapon was the sword, preferring to use the one which his father had handed down to him.

Kristal and Jaylon fought their way to Rebekah, killing the soldiers who tried to oppose them, and once they reached the princess they stood beside her. When the other knights reached Tabitha and Yosef, the soldiers dropped their swords and ran into the trees to try to escape. Following behind them were the hundred soldiers who had been following hard on the heels of the knights.

One of the eight was Seff. "Feliks, where is Shanna?" he asked. There was alarm in his voice.

Feliks couldn't see her at the large and wide tree. Without delay, he headed for the tree and started climbing it. He feared the worst.

"Shanna! Shanna! Where are you?" Feliks felt as if his heart had frozen.

"Here," a voice came from within the tree.

"She is here!"

Feliks was overjoyed.

No other soldiers were found in the woods.

When they returned to the castle, the king, who had been beside himself with worry, ran towards his daughters, hugging them in a tight embrace, not wanting to let go.

"Father!" Shanna objected. "You're making a spectacle!"

The king laughed.

Then he frowned as he saw Tabitha, Feliks and Yosef being treated for their wounds.

He was looking grave now.

"That's the last time you go into the woods," he said.

10

After the assault on the two princesses, Norandia had to deal with several small attacks, but all attempts to invade the kingdom were repelled. The king, worried about what was still to come, ordered his councillor to search for twelve men of stealth from within the villages.

"People of Norandia!" the councillor bellowed in each village square. "The king is looking for twelve courageous men who are willing to go beyond the walls of Norandia to find out what the enemy is up to."

Some of the villagers moaned. "Why doesn't the king use his own soldiers?" But they didn't know the king's intentions. He was looking for countrymen who could walk through the fields without attracting any attention, and who could draw near to the enemy camp without arousing any suspicion.

Searching for someone who would be willing to risk their life proved to be more difficult than the councillor expected, but after going through all the villages, he managed to gather at last twelve suitable men. Although they took some persuading, in the end they all agreed to the mission.

Once the men were briefed about the information they needed to acquire, they were sent on their way. These men appeared to all as ordinary country folk, with rough beards and baggy dark coloured clothes. However, beneath that rustic façade, there was cunning and skill.

The twelve men walked for days on end, passing through valleys where the green tones of their clothes caused them to merge into their surroundings. They were seen only by the wildlife, especially when they stopped to examine trees laden with juicy fruits. They stood beneath their lowering branches, pulling them down and tasting their juicy flesh.

"We will take some samples to the king on our way back," one of the soldiers said. "He might be interested in extending his kingdom here."

In the hours that followed, they were confronted by a wide river, which at that time of the year wasn't too deep. As they were crossing, they had to be careful where to put their feet. One unstable rock could cause them to lose their balance and fall into the cold water.

The scouting wasn't straightforward, but after exploring for twenty-one days, they found where the enemy had camped. The soldiers were spread out all over the valley. As soon as some of the men from Norandia saw this, they wanted to head back and give the bad news to the king, for they were discouraged by the size of the army. Others considered it normal to see so many men preparing for battle, and they managed to convince their colleagues, who decided to stay for a few more days to study their adversary.

The spies observed that the armour of the soldiers was black, with spikes on their chest and shoulders. Their helmets had three small pointed horns on their forehead, which made them look like demons. And their swords made the men tremble, for they were bigger than the ones that they had used in Norandia. There was a big bonfire in the centre of the camp where a sweaty blacksmith was making more of these weapons at alarming speed. He had gigantic arms and the work seemed effortless to him.

For the following two days, the spies studied the enemy camp, making use of the bushes and trees to hide themselves. On the second day, two of the men made use of the night to learn a bit more about their enemy, hiding outside what seemed to be the main tent. When they reached it, they made a small cut in its fabric so that they could see and hear what was being planned. Inside was Staffan's brother, Kidron, and some of his officers.

"We will commence the advance when the last group of men arrive," Kidron said.

"Sir, I have news." The words came from a soldier who had just entered the tent. "The men we are waiting for will be here tomorrow."

"In that case, we will start the march to Norandia in two days then," their leader said.

The two spies disappeared into the night, returning to their friends, where they shared the news.

The twelve spies started their journey back to their country without delay, only taking the shortest breaks to eat and rest. Their muscles were crying out with weariness and discomfort, but there was no time to attend to their own needs; their families and friends were in danger.

After many days of running, they saw the main tower of the castle in the distance. They summoned their last bit of strength and ran until they emerged from the great forest. The men were spotted by the watchmen in the watchtower, who informed the king of their return. Once the men passed through the castle gates, they fell to the ground, lying there exhausted and breathless. When the king arrived, they struggled as quickly as they could to their feet.

"My lord," one man gasped. "We have very little time. Your brother's forces will be coming from the south in about six days."

"Are they well-armed?" the king asked.

"Yes, my lord. We do not stand a chance against them in open battle. It will be better if we stay behind the walls."

This was not the news the king wanted to hear.

Seeing this, some of the spies began to argue. "Yes, but we have more experience than they have," one said.

"But they are stronger than us!" protested another. "We are like ants to them."

"Enough!" said the king. He turned to his chief councillor. "Send out some messengers."

"I will prepare the messengers straight away."

Then a general spoke. "My lord, we can position two hundred archers in the woods to halt their advance, and to protect those archers we can add three hundred soldiers with swords and spears."

"So be it," the king said. "Give the orders! We have very little time!"

11

As the warning bells began to sound throughout the kingdom, the people, fearing the worst, left everything they were doing to go to their homes and prepare for battle, leaving the fields and marketplaces empty. The children ran to their mothers, whilst the fathers and young men put on their fighting gear. The villagers were now, to all intents and purposes, the king's soldiers.

These soldiers gathered in the castle where they waited for instructions from their generals. All the soldiers were kept behind the walls of Norandia - all save several detachments which had been sent to the nearby woods from where a surprise enemy attack could easily be launched.

The king and the generals had been busy overseeing the preparations, but as the sixth day came to pass, time now ran out and they hoped that all that they had done was good enough. Staffan was nervous. He was moving backwards and forwards along the wall looking towards the south, expecting to see his brother at any time. And, as he gazed into the distance, there it was - a black line on the horizon, a vast column of enemy soldiers. The invasion was at hand.

"My lord," said one of the generals. "Five hundred men have been placed in the woods at the south of the kingdom, and the rest are behind the walls waiting for orders."

"How about the messengers?"

"I am afraid two have arrived with disturbing news. The kings they went to see have pledged allegiance to your brother."

"My lord," interrupted another soldier. "We have counted the enemy. We believe there are around three thousand men."

"Only three thousand?" asked the king.

The black line of soldiers now made a sudden stop. A small detachment of them advanced towards the walls of Norandia, pushing through their own front lines.

The archers behind the walls waited for the signal to let them know that the enemy was within shooting distance. As soon as the flag was waved, the archers tensed their bows and let go their arrows. Hundreds of arrows flew over the walls and covered the blue sky, casting a shade on the ground as they travelled towards their target.

There was a loud shout from the detachment and all the men came to an orderly halt, closed ranks, knelt and held their shields above their heads, forming a protective shell. When the arrows arrived, they clattered and broke against the shields, bouncing off and falling onto the ground.

As soon as the soldiers saw that the sky was clear, they reorganised and carried on walking. The archers promptly responded with a second volley of arrows. This time it was only a distraction. As soon as these arrows had travelled half their course and the soldiers had assumed the same defensive posture, two hundred arrows were released from the woods on their right flank.

The effect of these arrows was lethal. Most fell to the ground dying or dead. Some, more fortunate, survived, but they were shouting in pain. Only a few were fast enough to protect themselves.

"My lord," Seff said. "Something is not right. To conquer us they should be attacking us with their whole army."

"You are right," the king replied.

Three detachments now left the enemy lines. The first marched towards the walls of Norandia, the second towards the woods, and the third marched between the other two.

The first detachment carried on advancing, stopping whenever a wave of ferocious arrows came their way. On one occasion, the men were caught unguarded, as not long after only half a wave of arrows was sent, the second half followed as they were standing again without their shields raised. This caused many casualties, reducing the detachment in number.

The second detachment was cautious as they approached the woods. As soon as they safely reached the outlying trees, the third detachment changed direction and marched towards the woods as well.

"Send in the horsemen!" shouted the general.

When the horsemen charged into the woods they managed to put a halt to the enemy's advance before it had done too much damage to the king's archers within the forest. Nevertheless, the king lost many brave men. The remaining soldiers returned with the horsemen to the castle.

At that moment, the whole enemy army started to move forward with short deliberate steps, making the citizens of Norandia feel terrified. The king himself was concerned enough, but his sense of alarm was disturbed and momentarily suppressed by one of his own soldiers.

"My lord!" the man said. "The messengers have arrived and have brought reinforcements!"

The king looked towards the horizon and saw three different flags heading his way. The flags represented three of the different kingdoms he had approached for help. With them advancing, he no longer felt so isolated or alarmed. In fact, he was delighted at their loyalty towards him.

At that moment, something stranger happened. A loud trumpet sounded from behind the enemy lines. The oncoming soldiers stopped and started retreating. All the people in the kingdom shouted with joy, for they thought that they were victorious.

"Shall we follow them?" asked a general.

"No," the king replied. "It might be a trap."

As the sun set, the enemies of Norandia retreated. The battle had been brief, but intense. Since there was no more sign of Kidron's forces, the villagers were sent back to their homes.

Meanwhile, the king ordered several detachments of soldiers to conduct thorough searches throughout the kingdom before leaving sentinels to watch over the kingdom at night.

12

From his position on the wall, the king headed back to the castle escorted by ten knights, including Tytus and Tabitha. However, on the way, they were so taken up with the battle they had just witnessed they failed to notice what lurked in the shadows - thirty of Kidron's men who had somehow managed to get through a gap in the wall and were now intent on attacking the king.

The knights pulled Staffan behind them and took up a position in front of their king, facing the enemy. The thirty enemy soldiers now ran towards them with a loud battle cry. Tytus and Tabitha took their bows and managed to release as many arrows as they could, slaying five soldiers. As the enemy reached the knights, being far greater in number they broke the line that separated them from the king. Each knight was now on their own, embroiled in hand-to-hand and close quarter combat with at least double their number.

One knight, Shemuel, knew that simply deflecting his opponent's blade with his sword wasn't enough, so as soon as he felt free to manoeuvre, he grabbed one of his knives with his other hand and stabbed his adversary in the neck.

Shemuel was an average sized man but what he lacked in physical stature he more than made up for in his wisdom and learning. He would often recite all sorts of poems to his comrades. When he was in mortal combat, he would quote from the bards as he wielded his sword or cut and thrust at his enemy using the small collection of knives that he'd received from his father, who was a butcher, and which hung around his waist.

As Shemuel fought, he was heard uttering some lines: "You may be strong, but do not get me wrong, for it will not be long before you are gone, for I will use my cold and pointed knife to take away your life."

Everything was going well for Shemuel until a soldier knocked him onto his back. Just when he was about to be pierced by the man who struck him, Yosef jumped the soldier. An intense fight ensued in which both men were equal in strength, until Yosef anticipated the man's final move and knocked him out with one clean blow from his fist.

Tabitha was showing exceptional dexterity in evading her adversaries' lunges, until, that is, one of them tripped her. As she lost her balance, another soldier grabbed her around the neck and lifted her from the ground. Now she was struggling to breathe. Just when it seemed it was all over, Ahron managed to slice off the soldier's left arm with his sword.

Kislon, a short-haired robust knight who was comfortable using two small swords, was having difficulty suppressing the two soldiers with whom he was in combat, but a small error of judgment from one of them allowed him to redirect the man's sword into the heart of the other soldier. He then overcame the first assailant, cleverly escaping death. As he stood over the two corpses, several gashes became visible on his face and forehead, adding to the many he already had all over his body, evidence of a life full of fights and scraps. One scar spread right across his chest, and he would often show it to his comrades when asked, adding, "This is proof that even if you're involved in a fight that looks like you're almost certainly going to die, you can still live to fight another day!"

Another knight, Lisha, despite her lack of strength, was quick and agile, her lean frame and astute mind giving her an advantage. On this occasion, however, every time she received a blow she fell to the ground. Realising that she wasn't making any progress she changed tactics. As soon as she stood up, she took a few steps backwards to give herself enough space to jump with her sword lifted high. Both swords clashed noisily, but this time, instead of falling to the ground, she used her momentum to run behind the soldier, stabbing her opponent in the back, rage burning in her green eyes.

While all the knights were occupied, three enemy soldiers headed towards the king, surrounding and challenging him. Staffan tried to defend himself, but he ended up on the ground. The king was now immobilised, staring up at a soldier about to stab him in the chest. The growling man was about to apply the coup de grâce when Seff appeared with a roar and thrust his sword through the soldier's armpit, making him scream and fall.

The other two soldiers went to their friend's rescue, but Seff was ready for them. He grabbed his axe with his free hand and ran towards them. He parried the sword that was aimed at him by one soldier, then buried his axe head into the other man's side. In a split second, the first man was on top of Seff, enraged by the fatal wounds inflicted upon his comrades. Seff managed to kick him away, giving him enough time to swing his sword and cut the soldier's throat.

The king was safe, for the time being.

"My lord, are you all right?" Seff asked, proffering his hand, helping his king to his feet.

"Thanks to you, I am now!"

The surviving enemy soldiers were still superior in strength and height, but the noise of the fighting had raised the alarm for the king's personal bodyguards who came running to the knights' rescue, joining with them in a fight in which neither side was prepared to give quarter. After minutes of fighting, the intruders were lying on the blood-soaked ground.

They were dead.

But the king was alive.

"Long live the king!" the knights shouted.

When the hubbub died down, Shemuel spoke with his customary wisdom. "My lord," he said. "I believe the appearance of your brother was just a distraction so that these men could infiltrate the wall and try to assassinate you."

"It could be so," the king said.

Just then, Ahron cried out, "This one is still alive!"

The man was bleeding out a few yards away. He had lost one fight with the knights, and he was now losing another one, for survival. Shemuel leaned forward to interrogate him but he saw that blood was coming from the man's mouth. He knew that the wounded soldier didn't have much time left.

"Tell me," said Shemuel grabbing the man's hair. "How were you planning to let your generals know that you had killed the king?"

The man, who was now having difficulty in breathing, refused to speak. He simply shook his head. Then his face grew pale, his eyes lost their lustre, and he breathed his last.

This was the final casualty of the war between Kidron and Staffan. With the soldier's death, this was the last time the king and his knights saw or even heard anything from Kidron's men. To make sure that all was clear beyond the walls, Staffan sent out more spies, but they found no trace of the enemy. The battle was over, the feud was spent.

After burning the dead bodies and cleaning up their own wounds, the knights could at last sleep. It had been a long day and they deserved a rest.

Once again, Norandia was at peace.

13

There were no more wars after Staffan's brother retreated, and everything in Norandia went back to normality. However, the fact that Kidron wasn't showing any signs of life didn't mean that he had given up; in fact, he was developing a more sophisticated plan to seize the crown without losing any men. Staffan didn't know this, of course. He was enjoying a season of prosperity in his kingdom. The birth rate was increasing, and new barns were being built, full of grain.

As the years went by, the king's children grew, showing signs of increased maturity. Staffan knew that soon he would have to decide who would succeed him. There would come a time when he was old and unable to reign anymore. It was normal practice for the first son to take over, but after seeing how his sons were behaving, the king wasn't at all certain. All the boys had developed in different ways. Even though they were taught the same way, there were no two alike, and that didn't please the king at all.

Benjamen now had long brown hair which reached the nape of his neck, and brown eyes. In his teenage years, he had developed a proud character, believing that he would inherit his father's crown. Many times, when he was in class, he didn't understand what had been said, but he couldn't be bothered to ask. He lived for parties and fun and he knew that when he came out of the classroom his friends would be waiting for him to go out on the town. Staffan had placed him in charge of the fortress which watched over the lake, but whenever his father sent out a messenger for a report of how Benjamen was ruling it, he would be told that his son was hosting another party, wasting the resources of the fortress in riotous and indulgent living. Benjamen didn't worry about the cost of these parties; he believed the most important responsibility of being a king was to keep his people as happy as possible.

"Party!" shouted Benjamen at the end of every week.

"You are the best!" many would shout back.

Jakob, meanwhile, was different from his brother, for instead of being irresponsible with finances, he would organise his capital with wisdom, becoming richer and more prosperous. While he was in class, he would only think of the different ways of accumulating wealth. In this, he became more and more selfish, concerned only for his affairs and not for those of the kingdom. He was responsible for the fortress that took care of the crops, and his father was pleased with the reports that he was receiving, for he could see how his son was growing in wealth. But what Staffan didn't like was the fact that he was keeping all the money for himself.

One day, Jakob was daydreaming in class.

If I raise the tax and then build another barn, there would be more space to …

"Jakob, are you with us?" It was the teacher.

"Yes, of course."

"What did I just say then?"

Somehow Jakob could listen to the teacher at the same time as he was thinking about his own affairs, so he was able to answer.

Then, he went back to his own calculations.

Markus liked his hair very short, and due to all his rigorous training in the sun, he had a muscular and tanned body. He was a strong fighter, and he made sure that everybody in his fortress knew how to fight too. He enjoyed the classes with his brothers, but whenever he was asked a question, he went blank and didn't know how to respond. The simplest solution for him was to take his sword and stare into its blade whilst diverting the question to one of his brothers, or even to his father.

Staffan had placed him in charge of the fortress by the woods, and he was happy to hear how his son was training his people so that they could defend themselves from any invaders, but what worried him was that he couldn't resolve a matter within the kingdom.

"Markus, a villager needs your attention."

"What does he want?"

"Well, it's something to do with his neighbour not giving him back what is his."

Markus just rolled his eyes, placed his hand over his sword and said, "tell him to go and see my father. I am very busy."

As for Staffan himself, it was easier said than done getting a meeting with him because he had a busy schedule. He would have to wait days or even weeks to see the king. By that time the villager had become tired of waiting and come up with his own solution.

Luckas, a tanned young man, had the determination to learn all that he could from his father. He knew that he wouldn't become king, but that didn't stop him from doing his best in all that he did. He went to the same class as his brothers, but in contrast to them, after being dismissed he would search for shade under a tree and revise all that had been said that morning in the classroom.

Luckas was in charge of the fortress by the sea, and when Staffan was given reports of how his son was governing the surrounding area of the fortress he was content. Luckas wasn't just acquiring wealth through trading by the sea, he was also spending time with the villagers to find out about their concerns.

The king's daughters didn't have an important role looking after a fortress, for they lived in their father's castle. Instead, Rebekah and Shanna spent time with their mother learning all that they could in case they might become queen. She taught them good manners, how to be gentle but firm when needed, to be respectful, to know what to do in times of difficulties and to learn how to support their husbands. When they weren't with their mother they were with their father, observing how he resolved the matters that were brought to him, and when they weren't with their father they were shooting arrows and having fun.

Rebekah was going to marry soon and was going to live far away with the man she loved. Even though she was moving away, she still took part in the family's affairs, supporting her father whenever he had to make an important decision.

Shanna, on the other hand, was still young and enjoyed being carefree. She knew that ruling the kingdom wasn't going to be for her and that one day she would live in another castle with a prince who had asked for her hand in marriage. Trying to figure out what was going through her father's mind at that time in her life wasn't too much of a concern.

Staffan arranged a meeting with his children and went with them to have a picnic by the lake. It was a bright and warm day in which a gentle breeze stroked the branches of the trees, moving them backwards and forwards. The flowers around the lake clothed the green grass with a variety of vibrant colours, giving a cheerful welcome to anybody who passed near the lake. Not far from where the king had stopped with his children, some villagers decided to do the same, spending time together in the warmth of a family reunion. Six knights had left their heavy armour back at the castle and accompanied the king and his children to the lake, only carrying their weapons in case of danger. Shanna thought it was going to be a grown-up's conversation, so she decided to stay with them for a short while to show respect to her father, but as soon as she was able, she planned to find an excuse to leave them.

"Sons and daughters," started the king. "You all know why we are here, right?"

"Sure," answered Benjamen. "To talk about my approaching investiture."

Rebekah looked up and then to the lake. She couldn't believe how proud her brother had become. Staffan knew how delicate the matter was, so he spoke with love and chose the right words to avoid hurting their feelings.

"My son, I am afraid you have demonstrated that you cannot rule the part of the kingdom I have already given you. Even that responsibility I am now going to have to reconsider."

"What do you mean, father?" Benjamen wasn't sure where his

father was going with this.

Shanna rolled her eyes and huffed in disbelief. The others looked at her. "What?" she cried.

"Nothing, dear," Staffan said, shaking his head. "Well Benjamen, let us say that you do not use the kingdom's resources in the manner in which they should be used."

"Are you trying to say that…"

"He is saying that you are not fit to be king." It was Shanna who spoke, and everyone stared at her. "What? Did I say something wrong?" Shanna raised her left eyebrow. She liked to be direct, maybe too direct at times.

The king needed to remain serious, but inside he was laughing, for his youngest daughter had seen the mess her brother was causing while ruling over his fortress. Rebekah had to hide her face from her brothers for she couldn't contain her amusement. Then, when she managed to calm down, she looked at her sister and gave her a stern look, indicating that she was to behave herself.

"Is that true, father?" Benjamen asked, disturbed by the news.

"Yes, in a way it is."

"Father?" Shanna's eyes were wide open and full of innocence.

"Yes, my princess."

"Can I go for a little walk?"

"If that is what you want, yes." The king thought Shanna would cause less trouble away from the discussion.

"Tabitha!" the king said.

"My lord?"

"Go with Shanna and stay close to her."

"As you wish."

Shanna jumped and ran towards the flowers, stroking them with her hands as she walked through them. A butterfly caught her attention as she was skipping, so she dashed to try and catch it, but she wasn't being quick enough. The butterfly managed to fly over the lake, leaving Shanna way behind.

"Let me see, where were we?" The king squinted and looked at the lake while he recollected his thoughts. "Oh yes! Benjamen, as your sister has said, you have not demonstrated to me that you can act as a good king."

"But the villagers like it and they are happy."

"What would happen if all these resources ran out? Would they still be happy?"

Benjamen kept silent, for he was trying to think of ways to prove how wrong his father was.

"What about me?" Jakob saw an opportunity to become king. "We would be the wealthiest kingdom."

"Jakob, you do not share your wealth. Who would be wealthier, the kingdom or you?"

"What about me?" asked Markus. "We would force everyone to surrender at our feet." He finished by lifting his fist in the air.

"Markus, why do you treat everybody as your enemy?"

Benjamen was now annoyed and showing signs of frustration; he was desperate to become king. Jakob thought he could convince his father by giving him lots of numbers, and Markus just couldn't think of the appropriate words. Rebekah was silent, observing how three of her brothers were determined to be king, but in return they weren't willing to change. Luckas, meanwhile, was quiet too and listened in detail to all that was being said.

"You all have good points." said the king. "But good ruling is not just demonstrated by how content the people are, or by how wealthy you become, or even by how much you can impose fear over your lands. It is also about resolving matters in the right way without spending all your resources."

"But…" Benjamen tried to speak.

"No, I have heard enough." Then the king turned to the son who had remained silent. "But I would be interested in hearing what Luckas has to say. Why are you not arguing about becoming king?"

"Hahaha!" Jakob laughed. "He wouldn't be able to look after the kingdom even if he wanted to!"

Luckas smiled at his brother, and then looked at his father. "Father, I love you, and because I am the youngest I have no right to be king. In the same way I have served you, I will serve whoever becomes king."

"That is good to know," Benjamen said.

"Silence!" Staffan was beginning to lose his patience. "Your brother's way of ruling his fortress is far better than yours!"

Benjamen did not look happy at that.

At that moment, not far from where they were having their picnic, a small cloud of dust began to rise from the pathway. It was one of the king's castle guards galloping at full speed towards them.

"My lord!" shouted the guard as soon as he had eye contact with the king. "Two villagers and their servants are fighting over some cows in the south of the kingdom."

"Can they not wait for a few days?" The king didn't want to be disturbed.

"I am afraid not, my lord. According to what they say they wanted to speak with your son a while ago, but he said that he was too busy to attend to them. They want their cows back now, but we don't know who to give what since both claim to be the legitimate owner."

The king thought for a moment as he looked at his sons and then at Rebekah. She knew what her father was thinking. Shanna, who was picking flowers, was called back; it was time to leave.

"Take us to the villagers," the king said to the guard. Then he looked at his sons. "When we are there, my sons will be the ones who resolve the dispute and make the decision."

Everyone mounted their horses and headed south with the guard leading the way. As they drew nearer, they could see a crowd of people being kept in order by some soldiers. It wasn't just the people involved in the dispute who were there. Villagers from the surrounding hamlets had rushed to the scene having heard about the argument.

As the king and his children approached, the soldiers formed a cordon around the two owners, keeping the servants and neighbours away and leaving plenty of space for the king.

"My sons will be the ones who will adjudicate this matter."

The two disgruntled villagers bowed.

"You start by telling your version," said the king as he pointed at the man standing on the right.

"My lord, we both own a herd of cows. One day three of my cows went to this man's property to graze. He is now claiming that the cows are his and he will not give them back to me."

"Now you." The king pointed at the man on the left.

"My lord, I agree that we both have cows, but these cows have always been mine. I know my own cows better than he knows his own."

"Liar!"

"Silence!" shouted the king. "My sons will decide what to do."

Benjamen looked at all the people. He knew how to please them, and he was going to prove his father wrong. He then looked at the two villagers and then to his brothers. He was sure he was wiser than them.

"You both claim that the cows are yours, and because you cannot come to an agreement, I command that you kill them, cook them and prepare a feast for the villagers."

Behind the protective cordon that the soldiers had made, several villagers shouted support for what Benjamen had said. The two villagers protested, however; both knew that there would be no profit for them.

Shanna rolled her eyes and placed her hands on her waist. "When will this boy grow up?" she mumbled.

Staffan wasn't surprised by what he heard, but even so he accepted his son's proposition.

"I do not think the same as my brother." Jakob now spoke. He too wanted to impress his father. "I will sell the cows, and from the profit that I make, half will be for the two villagers and the other half for the king."

The two villagers were unhappy with that decision as well. The king said nothing. He looked at Rebekah, who didn't seem to have been convinced by either of the answers given so far.

"I will give one cow each," Markus said. "And the one that is left will be for the king, for forcing him to come here and for wasting his time."

Markus looked surprised at the wisdom that had poured out of his mouth, as if he had spoken before he had thought. Staffan nodded with satisfaction at him. Markus' solution was far better.

Luckas moved closer to the cows and studied them. The people were curious and observed him in silence. He noticed that two of the cows were old, whereas the third one was still young. *My brother Markus has given a pretty good ruling, but he still wouldn't be able to know who the real owner was.*

"My brothers have given good advice, but by doing what they have suggested we would never find out the truth. So, I suggest the old cows are given back to the villagers, having one each, but as for the young one, I will order Seff to come and cut it in half."

While waiting for his father's answer, Luckas could hear the villagers mumbling. He then looked at Rebekah, who was looking at him while raising her left eyebrow, and at Shanna, whose eyes seemed to want to pop out from their sockets. When he finished scrutinizing his siblings, he looked at his father, who in turn looked at Seff and nodded.

"Move aside," Luckas said. "There's going to be blood everywhere."

Seff stopped in front of the cow and lifted his sword. He gave a loud shout and prepared to bring the blade down upon the creature's back.

One of the villagers then gave a cry and knelt in front of Luckas, pleading for mercy for the cow.

"Please, my lord! Have mercy on her. She is still young. Rather than kill her, just give her alive to my neighbour."

"I don't care whether the animal lives or dies," said the other villager. "Just carry on and give me the best half."

"Stop!" Luckas ordered. "There is no need to divide the cow. Only the real owner would have asked for mercy for the young animal!"

Everybody voiced their approval at his judgement. Staffan nodded; his youngest son had given the right answer. He then looked at Rebekah who smiled with approval towards her brother. She seemed delighted with him, and Shanna was overjoyed at how the villagers had accepted his answer.

His brothers, on the other hand, were fuming, jealous of Luckas and the way everybody was congratulating him.

Luckas continued. "To prevent this from ever happening again, you will construct a wall between the two properties. You will both contribute to the work and you will both pay all the expenses."

"But, my lord!" the guilty villager cried. But he was interrupted by the king.

"Would you rather die?"

"No, my lord."

Everybody now went back to their own house, talking of how wise Luckas had been as a judge.

Meanwhile, since their presence wasn't needed anymore, the king and his children headed back to the castle, escorted by the knights.

15

Luckas had a lot to learn before the investiture, so he stayed close to his father, learning everything that he could. Everyone was happy for Luckas - everyone except Benjamen, whose veins were poisoned by envy. He didn't take kindly to the fact that his youngest brother was going to become king of Norandia. He had resolved to do something about it.

One night, during the late hours, two hooded men lurked in the shadows, whispering to each other at the walls that protected the kingdom. Their whispers were lost in the loud whistling of the wind.

These two men had met several times before in the same location and nobody had ever noticed their presence. During those meetings, the men exchanged vital information about the kingdom.

One of those men was Benjamen.

"Tell me, what is your father up to now?" asked the man.

"He has told me he will name Luckas."

"That cannot be possible. You are the first born."

"That is what I have told him, but he will not listen to me."

"He is a fool."

"What can I do?"

"If you swear loyalty to me, I will give you advice," said the man. He was grinning beneath his cowl.

"Fine!" Benjamen said. "But I will be the one who rules over Norandia."

"Of course. But remember, power corrupts."

"I can handle it. Now tell me, what must I do?"

"You must kill Luckas."

"Kill him?!" His whisper had turned into a shout.

Benjamen realized he had spoken louder than he should have done, so he kept quiet. The guards were not far away, inspecting the walls as part of their nightly patrols. It was clear that they had heard something, for they stopped and shone their torches around. As they couldn't see anything, the two guards turned around and then continued.

"Yes, kill him, unless you want to serve him for the rest of your life!"

"Never!" Benjamen hissed.

"You must kill him, then. But first, you must convince your other two brothers about what you are planning to do."

"What do you get out of all this?" Benjamen asked.

"You will know nearer the time, but now I must depart."

The man headed away from the wall, while Benjamen headed back to the castle where he managed to convince Jakob. Neither wanted to submit to their youngest brother. Now they needed to convince Markus.

16

The three brothers headed towards one of the forests not far from Benjamen's fortress. As they entered the forest, what they didn't realise was that somebody had spotted them from a distance and was following them.

The brothers advanced deep into the woodland, through the dense vegetation, moving the branches aside from their path. It didn't take them long to arrive at an open space surrounded by trees and bushes.

"Markus, the reason we have brought you here is because we want to talk to you about our brother," started Jakob.

"What about him?" Markus was intrigued.

"Come on! Do not act as if you do not care!" Benjamen cried.

"Calm down Benjamen!" Jakob knew how to deal with his brother. "Markus, Luckas is the youngest and we cannot allow him to be king. Are you prepared to serve your baby brother? It should be the other way around!"

"What are you suggesting?" asked Markus.

"Kill him!" Benjamen was showing his teeth as he snarled. "I will be the king, and you two will be allowed to do anything you want in my kingdom."

"What makes you think father will choose you?" asked Markus.

"Because I am the oldest!"

"But kill your own brother? Benjamen, he is our brother."

"I do not care! Are you with us or against us? If you are not up to it, I know of someone who is. I spoke with him not long ago and we have decided it is the best solution."

"You never told me this," said Jakob turning to Benjamen in surprise.

"You do not need to know everything."

"What do you suggest then, Markus?" Jakob asked.

Just then the bushes started to move. The brothers gave a quick glance at their surroundings. They were trapped, encircled by bushes full of thorns. Their hearts felt as if they were beating in their throats.

Has someone heard our conversation?

Benjamen was in distress, and his eyes were dancing whilst scanning his surroundings.

Markus held his sword and waited.

"Brothers!" shouted Luckas. "What are you doing here? I saw you from a distance and followed you. This is a nice place."

This could not have worked out any better.

Benjamen was smiling.

Luckas stepped out of the shadows and walked towards Markus. While he was distracted, Benjamen managed to slide behind him, and dealt Luckas a severe blow to the back of his head, leaving him unconscious on the ground.

Markus was shocked. Only now did he realise how serious his brothers were. The idea of killing a member of the family was making him feel very uncomfortable. He had to find another solution.

Just at that moment he became aware of a noise at the edge of the forest and went to see what was happening. He noticed that there was a large caravan of travellers passing by and an idea flashed in his head. Rushing back, he cried out, "Wait! Don't kill him. I understand he is a rival, but he is our brother, right?"

"And what do you propose then?" Benjamen asked, lowering his knife.

"We get rid of him."

"That is what I was trying to do!"

"Not by killing him."

"How then?"

"We sell him," Markus said.

"I like it!" Jakob shouted.

"How are we going to do that?" Benjamen asked.

"I remember father telling me that beyond this forest there is a trade route, where caravans of merchants pass from one territory to another. There's one passing by right now. We might be able to sell Luckas to them as a slave."

"But what do we say to father?" asked Jakob.

Benjamen answered. "We will tell him that we were in the forest when some wolves caught us by surprise and attacked and killed him. All we need to do is remove his clothes and soak them in blood."

"You can be in charge of that," Markus said. "And do not forget to take his medallion."

"And you, Jakob, can be our spokesman with the traders," Benjamen said.

Jakob ran to catch up with the caravan. He made it to the tail of the convoy, whereupon he started his search. Several armed men looked at him with suspicion as he walked towards the front of the convoy. However, once he reached the front, he found the slave owner.

"May I have an audience with you, sir?" Jakob asked, placing both his hands together in front of his chest in respect.

The man paid no attention.

"We have a ..." Jakob paused. He was about to refer to his brother. "We have a worker who is of no more use to us, and we thought you might want him."

"What makes you think that?"

"He is young."

"Where is he?"

Benjamen and Markus were even now dragging their brother, still unconscious, towards the convoy. It took the two brothers longer than expected to reach the front, where the owner had begun to become impatient. The man had a schedule to meet and couldn't lose any more time.

On their arrival, he started to examine Luckas in detail, for people had tricked him before and he wasn't prepared for that to happen again. The man looked at the boy's skin; it was healthy with no sign of him being beaten anywhere. He slid his finger through the boy's hair to feel its strength, checked his chin and opened his eyelids. Everything seemed to be there.

The man took a small mirror from his pocket and placed it under Luckas' nose.

"Well, at least he's still alive," he said. He took hold of the boy's palms and looked at them. "Not the hands of a worker," he muttered. He touched the boy's legs and counted his toes. "All there," he mumbled.

"Looks a bit like you two," he said.

"Just a coincidence," Benjamen said. "What are you offering?"

"Thirty pieces of silver," said the man.

"He's young," Benjamen said. "Forty-five."

"You have held me up," the merchant said. "I should be offering twenty."

"Very well, thirty then. It is a good number," said Jakob, fearing that he would lower his offer even more.

The man headed towards his horse and took a bag and withdrew the money while the brothers grabbed Luckas under his arms and pulled him towards a wooden cart, whereupon the trader and his caravan recommenced their journey.

The brothers stood and watched the merchants disappearing behind the hills, knowing it was the last time that they would ever see their brother again.

"Time to go hunting," said Markus, breaking the silence.

Markus had been given the task of searching for a deer, his hunting skills being far better than his brothers. Once he had killed one, he gave it to Benjamen, who cut open the animal's side to soak Luckas' clothes in its warm and sticky blood. It wasn't a pleasant job, but if they wanted to make their story convincing they had to get their hands dirty.

Once the clothes were shredded and soaked, they hid the deer behind a bush and covered it with several branches. They then washed their hands in a nearby stream.

They then returned to the castle to convey the news to their father that his youngest son had been mauled to death and carried off by wolves. When the king was informed, he was speechless with shock and grabbed the armrest of his throne. The tragic report spread fast, and the whole kingdom joined Staffan in his grief. In desperation, the king was observed watching from his balcony during the day, hoping to see his son beyond the walls of Norandia. Until hope began to evaporate altogether like a morning mist.

Without a dead body to prove the three brothers' story, Seff went out to explore. There was something about their account which made him doubt their version of what had happened. The knight searched in the forest, but he found no trace of blood. He then decided to extend the search for a week. He arrived at a spot that looked suspicious. Several broken branches caught his attention, and closer examination revealed that the branches had been cut on purpose. His attention was then drawn to what seemed to be a bush covered with dry leaves. As he moved the branches away, a strong odour made him recoil. Whatever it was, it was clearly decomposing, so he placed a cloth over his nose and mouth. The next moment, he discovered a dear killed by a cut to the throat, not by the attack of a predator, such as a wolf.

Seff could now form a picture of what had happened, but he could not prove it. Sharing his reconstruction of events with the king would just cause him even more distress. Furthermore, if he labelled the king's sons as liars he could be punished, so he kept the whole matter to himself.

For the time being, at least.

17

Luckas moaned in pain as he regained consciousness. He was shivering with cold. When he opened his eyes, he discovered why: some of his clothes were missing. To his even greater surprise, he found himself shackled inside a small cage. As he tried to work out where he was, the last thing he could remember was speaking to his brother Markus, and after that everything was unclear. As he looked around, he saw other men like him in the cage, wearing old rags as clothes.

"How did I get here?"

"Two men pulled you out from a forest," said one of them.

"Who?"

The man shrugged his shoulders.

Luckas shouted for help, but all his attempts were in vain; nobody came to his rescue. He put his head in his hands. When, a short time later, a man came to give them some food, Luckas tried to have a conversation with him, but his questions were ignored.

Days went by, and those days turned into weeks, until Luckas had lost all track of the passing of time.

Then, one morning, waking from his sleep, he was shocked to see people outside the cage staring at him and at his travelling partners. He didn't know where he was, but he felt relieved to see signs of civilisation. They had stopped at a square, and they were surrounded by what looked like wealthy householders wanting to buy slaves. With dawning realisation at what was about to happen to him, Luckas began to panic. He tried to call out for help several times, but that just stirred the people to make fun of him.

"Be quiet!" the merchant said.

"I should not be here. This is a mistake!"

"You make me laugh, boy."

"But my father is a king!" Luckas felt for his medallion as he cried. But all he found was his own skin. He had nothing to prove his identity.

"I said, be quiet and behave yourself, or else."

Luckas wanted to escape but he knew that nobody would help him. He was now in a slave market in a strange city in an unfamiliar country. He felt alone and miserable, and a deep sadness was sinking into his soul. He no longer saw any point in resisting. The other people in the cage seemed to have simply resigned themselves to their fate as well. There was no fight in them at all.

In what followed, the buyers touched the slaves before they bid. The slaves were placed in a line and the prospective buyers walked around them, prodding their arms and legs, making sure that they were fit and in good health.

Every time anybody attempted to touch him, Luckas tried to move away. The merchant's helper, annoyed at what he was seeing, reached for his whip and headed towards him. He lifted the whip and was about to hit him when the merchant stopped him.

"Do not harm this one!"

"Yes sir," said the assistant.

The time for bidding time arrived and Luckas was led to a wooden platform where he could be seen by the buyers. Due to his heavy chains, he ascended the stairs with difficulty. Once on the platform, he saw a crowd of people waiting for him. The sight made his thoughts travel to the past, where he was presented to a larger multitude as a prince and not as a slave. It filled him with a great melancholy to think that he would belong to someone. There was no chance of running away. The chains bound him fast.

"Smile a bit, son. You need to make me some money," said the merchant.

Luckas tried to produce a fake smile but it was hard for him to show any sign of happiness at such a horrific moment.

During the bidding that followed, some men tried to outbid one another for the boy. It was intense, and the people around them were enjoying it. The bidding started with thirty pieces of silver.

"Thirty-five!" said a man at the front.

"Forty!" shouted another one.

"Forty and a cow!" joined in another man.

The merchant was rubbing his hands. The foreign boy was making him good money.

When it seemed that the bidding was about to finish, an old grey-haired and bearded man with a big belly gave the final push.

"Fifty pieces of silver!"

"Sold to the man on the right!" shouted the merchant with undisguised joy.

Luckas' buyer, it turned out, was a very wealthy man and the reason why nobody dared to raise their bid was because they knew that he could easily outdo them. Furthermore, he wasn't a pleasant man to have as a rival. He was a well-known landowner who had many acres of fields which produced a large amount of crops from forced labour. Now, the old man, content with his purchase, paid the price and grabbed Luckas, taking him to his horse and cart where one of his sons was waiting.

They had to travel for several hours through the countryside to the place where the old man lived. The fields were green and adorned with beautiful flowers, but for Luckas that meant nothing.

All he could see were different tones of grey.

Luckas said nothing during the journey, observing his surroundings as he tried to figure out where he was. When they arrived at the man's house, Luckas observed the condition of his slaves, knowing that soon he would become like them. His heart sank; they looked thin and exhausted.

The cart stopped in front of a wooden house, where a bearded man with a long wooden stick was waiting at the door. He was smiling, for he enjoyed instructing new people. The part he enjoyed the most was hitting them if they didn't obey.

"This man will teach you how to do things around here," said the old man. "You'd better take careful notice of what he says, or else he will have just cause to punish you."

Luckas gave the man a glance but said nothing.

"Come this way," said the old man.

They walked through a narrow corridor which led to a chamber inside the house. The room had a wooden table in the middle, barely visible in the insufficient light from a small crackling fire. The two windows had been covered with planks of wood. Luckas felt shivers when he made out the heads of four stuffed deer hanging on the walls as trophies.

Two men grabbed the young man by force and laid him on the table. Luckas tried to kick them, but the more resistance he offered, the more brutal they were with him. He was now lying face down on the table and couldn't move. He shouted for help, but nobody came to his rescue. Tears were dropping from his cheeks and he wished he was dead.

Another man stepped forward from the shadow and stood beside Luckas with a hot iron bar that had an "S" figure at the end. The young man tried to move away, but he couldn't.

There was nothing he could do to prevent what happened next.

Luckas screamed as the metal bar savaged the skin on his right shoulder. The pain was so intense that he fell unconscious, staying that way for the rest of the day.

During his first weeks, Luckas tried to escape, but all his attempts were useless, for he was discovered and later punished, having several scars on his back to prove it. If the slaves were good and didn't try to flee, their chains were removed, a far more comfortable condition.

After several months, Luckas gave up his attempts to escape, and as a result, life became very monotonous. In the mornings, he struggled to rise from his bed, but once he was on his feet, he went to wash himself with cold water. The water was changed at night, so those who got there first had clean water, but the latecomers had to content themselves in water which had already been used, or they were sent to a nearby river. After washing, they had to run to the kitchen; if they weren't at the table at a set time, the food would be taken away from them. Breakfast consisted of two slices of bread and a glass of milk, but twice a week they would be given a cooked breakfast, which was what they enjoyed the most.

After breakfast, the slaves were guided to a field where they worked all morning. At midday, they were given a short break and some food. This was the part of the day which Luckas enjoyed the most, for if it was sunny, which it was most days, he would eat sitting under a tree. If he ate quickly, he would manage to sleep a little.

After the break, they had to go to another field that needed their attention, and if they finished too soon, they were taken to the village to purchase provisions for the house.

Dinner consisted of a glass of water and two slices of bread, but there were three days a week when they were given some vegetables accompanied by a juicy piece of steak. They were never given enough food, and that is why the slaves were always hungry, but they didn't dare complain, because if they did, they would receive no food for twenty-four hours.

At the end of the day, after all their hard work, they crawled into bed, curling up inside the sheets with aching joints and muscles.

Luckas had tried to convince the men several times that he was a prince, but the more he did it, the more fun they made of him. They nicknamed him "the Prince", but they never treated him like one.

By now, Luckas was skinny and weary. As time had gone by, his hopes of seeing any familiar faces had faded to the point where he thought that his family were happier and better off without him.

One day, whilst Luckas was on one of his short breaks, the old man stood in front of him, blocking his view.

"Hey prince," said the old man.

"Yes, master."

"I want you to go now to the village."

"Yes, master."

"And when you return, I want you to clean my shoes."

"Yes, master."

"Hey prince! Where is your father now?!" said the old man's son enjoying the moment.

Luckas didn't have the strength to argue, so he looked down in shame and obeyed. He walked to the village escorted by a man who wouldn't hesitate to whip him if he tried to escape. It took them several hours to buy all that the old man had asked for, and once he had it all he headed to his master's house carrying a heavy load through a crowded market. There were stalls situated all along the main street, and the people were busy buying and selling. It was hectic, but somehow, among all the people that were walking and pushing on their way to the next stall, the young prince saw a familiar face not far from where he was standing. He stood still and stared at him. At first, he thought that he was imagining things, but as he closed his eyes several times to confirm what he had seen, he realized that it was Seff, so he tried to call his attention.

"Seff!" shouted Luckas in a very weak voice that could only be heard by the man who walked besides him.

"What is it that you said, prince?"

"Seff!" tried Luckas again.

"My name is not Seff!" said the man using his whip.

Seff and Luckas stared at each other, but the knight didn't recognise him. Life as a slave had changed his appearance. A horse and cart rode between them, blocking their eye contact, and when it had moved on, Seff was no longer on the other side.

Luckas cried, his tears running down his cheeks, dropping onto his bare and sore feet.

As far as he was concerned, that was his last chance of returning home.

18

It was a year since Luckas had been bought as a slave, and his living conditions hadn't improved. To try to exhaust him even more, his master made him work in the barn at night. One evening, as he walked towards his tent after finishing his tasks, he saw how one of the slaves was being beaten in a backyard. He was exhausted, but he had to try to stop the man.

To avoid being noticed, he moved in the shadows. As he walked by the old man's house, he peered through the window and saw the old man counting his money while fiddling with his beard. Luckas didn't allow himself to be distracted by the money, so he carried on walking and stayed at the corner of the house, waiting for a clear moment to help the slave.

"You will think twice before you do that again!" said the man who was beating the slave.

"Yes master. I am sorry... I will not do it again."

"Sir," interrupted Luckas. "You should stop beating him. He has had enough."

"Who are you? Let me see your face."

"I am Luckas."

"Oh! It is the prince! So, you think that I should stop?"

"Yes, sir."

The man lifted the stick to hit Luckas but the young prince found the strength to fend it off with both hands.

"Fool! You will go hungry for this!"

Luckas didn't reply. He had to act fast before anyone came to see what all the commotion was about, so he pulled the stick backwards and knocked the man on his nose, causing it to bleed. The man thrust his right hand over his nose and felt the sticky blood running down the side of his mouth.

"How dare you!"

Luckas grabbed the stick and struck the man until he fell on his knees. Now that he was defenceless, he changed his tone, and instead of commanding Luckas to stop, he switched to a pleading tone.

"Prince! Stop! I said stop! Have mercy... no more."

The young prince didn't relent; he carried on striking the man. One final blow rendered the man fall unconscious. When Luckas had realized what he had done he dropped the stick and ran away.

"Wait!" said the other slave. "Do not leave me here!"

But fear had overcome the young prince. He ran like he had never done before, forgetting about the slave he had gone to rescue. His feet were sore, but he only had one thought, to disappear from the scene, so he ran and ran, not looking behind.

Luckas dashed into a nearby forest. Half of his weary heart was elated to be free; the other half was sorry to have left others behind. After running for several hours his whole body was throbbing in pain, but he couldn't stop now, not after what he had done.

At one point he found himself hurtling downhill and he lost control of his weak legs and fell to the ground, rolling all the way down to the bottom. It felt like it was a never-ending fall, and then, it all stopped.

Luckas looked around to try to orientate himself, but there wasn't enough light. All he could see was the reflection of the moon on a nearby lake. He tried to crawl, but since his body was aching and he was finding it hard to move, he gave himself some time to rest and closed his eyes.

19

The sun had been out for several hours and was warming everything within its reach. The birds welcomed the bright and sunny morning and Luckas woke up to their singing. Straight away he felt intense pain throbbing through his body. As he opened his eyes, he saw a young woman in a dark blue dress staring into his eyes. Her auburn brown hair was plaited around her head. He looked at her half smiling.

Am I in heaven?

How can that be?

I am still so young.

Luckas didn't utter a word, but instead gave a quick glance at his surroundings. However, everything except for this mysterious woman was blurred; his eyes hadn't yet adapted to the unusual brightness of the light. The colours around him were too vivid for his pupils, still acclimatising to the daylight. The only person he could see was the young woman staring at him. As he looked at her again, she started to smile. Luckas was shocked and attempted to escape by moving backwards using his arms and legs.

Luckas was now convinced that all this was a trap designed to take him back to the old man, so he had to try to escape. His body hadn't healed during the night and it was wracked with pain, but he managed to move away in the hope of escaping from her presence, but he didn't see the tree that was behind him. Knocking his head against the bark, he winced, gave up, and sat dismayed upon the ground. As he did, his eyes drooped, and he fell once again into a deep sleep.

The second time the young prince woke up, he noticed that the surface he was lying on wasn't as hard as it had been in the forest. With his eyes still shut, he extended his hand and touched the material, feeling a soft surface, which made him think that he was on a bed. His suspicions made sense when he opened his eyes, for he saw a roof above him, a big window to his right, and in front of him a door, with two big wardrobes next to it. When he turned his head to the left he was surprised to see the same woman from the forest sitting on a sofa and watching every move he made. Luckas froze as he stared at her, not knowing what to do.

"Where am I?"

"You are in our guest room," said the young woman. "My father does not allow villagers to enter this room, which is for royal guests, but he has made an exception for you."

Luckas looked beneath the sheets and saw that he was wearing clothes that didn't belong to him, not the rags he had been wearing before he fainted.

"They are my brother's," the young woman laughed as she spoke and placed her hand over her mouth.

Intrigued by her kindness, the young prince continued questioning.

"Your father's guest room? Am I dreaming?"

"Calm down, my mysterious villager," she said with a smile. "You are not dreaming."

"I am not a villager," Luckas said. "I am a prince."

"You did not look like a prince," she said as she pointed to a chair where his old clothes were hanging.

"Did you... did you ... undress ..."

"Oh no! Some servants did."

Luckas tried to reach out to touch the scar on his right shoulder.

It had been covered with some sort of dressing.

"They also tended to your wounds." The woman paused. "You were not treated well as a slave, were you?"

He could tell that she had seen the branding on his body.

"How long have I been sleeping?" he asked, changing the subject.

"Two days, but do not worry. My father will not seek reparation."

"So, who is your father?"

"My father is the King of Zophrandia."

"Please forgive my impertinence, but Zoph… what?"

"Zophrandia, one of the kingdoms of the northern territories."

Luckas remembered what he had been taught. "There are four kingdoms in the northern territories, right?" he asked.

"There are only three now. My father wanted to expand his kingdom, so he conquered one of them." She started walking towards the window. "Everything that you can see from here belongs to my father. I found you while walking in one of my father's many gardens. You were very badly hurt." She turned towards him when she said this, her eyes filled with pity.

For Luckas, this was all too much and he now needed to breathe fresh air, so he got out of bed and headed towards the window. As he did, he realised he was no longer in pain. The scars were still there, and his heart was still troubled by what he'd been through, but he was pain free. As he looked out of the window he couldn't believe the vast extent of the land. The castle was enormous, and a large wall surrounded it on all sides. To the left, he could see the ocean. Beneath him, he could see a marketplace where villagers were selling their products. In the distance, he could see soldiers training in an open space, using moves that he hadn't used for a long time.

Luckas now realized that all this wasn't a dream. The woman he was talking to was clearly a princess and had saved him from an almost certain death.

Remembering his manners, he exclaimed, "How rude of me! I have not told you my name. I am Luckas."

"And my name is Abigail."

With that, the door opened and one of the princess' maidservants, a blonde and middle-aged woman, entered in a rush. She observed the young man with suspicion before she spoke. "Abigail, your father wants you."

"Very well, I will come now."

As Abigail was walking towards the door, Luckas seized his opportunity. "Would it be possible to speak with your father?" he asked.

"I will see what I can do," said Abigail as she walked out of the room.

The maidservant walked just behind her and gave him a quick glance before closing the door.

Several hours went by and Luckas heard nothing from the princess. He didn't have anything to do in the room, so he just lay on the bed and waited. As time passed by, his stomach began to inform him that it was dinner time. Just then, the same maidservant appeared with the food on a tray. She seemed annoyed by his presence.

"Here's your dinner."

"Thank you," said Luckas. "Is there any news?"

"What about?" she asked as she placed the tray on a table.

"My request to speak to the king."

"I have heard nothing, but then I am just a maidservant."

"Where is Abigail?"

"That's not your concern."

"I am sorry if my presence is not welcome," Luckas said. "I will go as soon as I can."

"I hope so," she replied.

To avoid annoying her anymore, Luckas kept his mouth shut and watched her go, closing the door behind her and leaving him alone to enjoy his warm meal, the delicious food bringing life back to his body. After wiping the dish with bread, he climbed back into bed. This was not the time for exploring the castle. If he was caught, they might stop being so kind and generous with him.

A short while later, Luckas was about to fall asleep when the door burst open and two men with lighted candles entered his room. They stood right next to his bed.

"Son," said one man. "You had better get up."

"Why?"

"You want to see the king, right?"

"Yes."

"Well, we have to measure you first and then make you some decent clothes. You need to look presentable."

Luckas complied without objections. When he got out of bed, the other man opened his arms and took his measurements whilst the first shone a light on what his colleague was doing. Due to the weakness of the light, Luckas couldn't tell who the men were, but he knew that they were tailors, for they were doing their job with precision.

As soon as some fabric was brought to the room in a box by two new men, the four of them worked as a team. While two were holding candles to light up their work, the other two were stitching everything together. They worked so swiftly and efficiently that

Luckas' clothes were ready in just two hours.

Once everything was finished, the men observed their masterpiece in silence before walking out of the room, leaving Luckas alone to try on his long white sleeved shirt with his green waistcoat. He then bent down to put on his black baggy trousers. To finish off the outfit, he slipped on his knee-high black boots which took longer than expected to tie up. He then stepped closer to the mirror to check his outfit. He loved it.

The following morning, Luckas was taken by two soldiers to the king's courtroom, walking along several long passages before arriving at the door. Once inside, he noticed that there were sentries standing next to each column in the chamber. From a distance it appeared that the king was accompanied by several generals and two of his advisers. He knew he was the king because he was wearing a golden crown over his blond hair. The man looked healthy and fit, his body rippling with muscles. Luckas reckoned he was a formidable fighter, for he saw four large statues of mighty warriors standing on guard at the end of the room. Rays of light poured onto them from enormous windows above which allowed natural light to enter. When it was dark, the chamber would be illuminated by the lampstands in every corner and three big lamps which hung from the roof with a dozen candles in each.

As Luckas began to ascend the three step stairs to approach the king, two guards aimed their spears at his chest, not allowing him to walk any further. Standing where he was, Luckas was aware of the king's penetrating stare. He felt as if the man was reading the inner part of his soul.

Seeing that he wasn't going to be allowed any closer, he knelt and bowed in reverence.

"I have been told you wanted to see me," the king said, his sonorous voice echoing around the hall.

"My lord," Luckas said. "First of all, I want to thank you for your generosity and kindness by allowing me to stay until I am well."

"You are welcome, though you must know that it was my daughter who did it all. If it had been up to me, I would have left you out in the cold."

"I am grateful to your daughter, then."

"What can I do for you?" the king asked.

"Your daughter told me that we are in the northern territories, and if I am right, it will be a long journey on horseback to return to my father's castle. Is that correct, my lord?"

The king started laughing, as did, all the other men present. It seemed that Luckas wasn't to be given an answer.

When the laughter died down, the king spoke. "What is your name, son?"

"Luckas, your majesty."

"And what do you want?"

"A boat, my lord, to return home."

"Do you know how much a boat would cost you? Would you not rather have a horse?"

Luckas had thought about that. If he travelled by horse, he would have to ride by one of his brothers' fortresses, which meant that if it was them who had sold him as a slave, they would do anything to stop him from returning to Norandia. He also assumed that they would have informed the guards and soldiers to forbid the entrance of anybody who claimed to be Luckas.

On the other hand, going by boat would mean that he would be able to go via the fortress by the sea, and because it had been under his control, he would have more chance of knowing the guards on duty. He also calculated the timescale; he knew that his father wasn't in a hurry to name Benjamen as his successor, and that he would try to delay it for as long as possible. Also, before this could take place, his brother would have to be trained. So, presuming that he had plenty of time, he chose the most appropriate option.

"My lord, the sea is the best option," Luckas said.

The king looked at the men next to him to see if they had anything to add. One of them stepped forward and whispered something into his ear.

"This is my decision," the king then said. "You will work for me for a year, and I will pay you by giving you the materials you will need for the boat. You will live in a village next to the ocean, and in that way, you can be close to your boat... If by any means you try to betray me, you will be executed. Do you agree with these terms?"

"Yes," said Luckas, who in truth had no other option. Then he said, "My lord, may I know my masters name?"

"My name is Cyrenius," said the king.

"It is a pleasure," the prince said.

"The pleasure is all mine!" The king replied, placing his arm around the young man's shoulders before taking him on a tour of his castle.

The following day, Luckas was taken to the house of the family he was going to stay with while he worked for the king. The house, near the seashore, was small, but it had a warm and welcoming atmosphere. The moment he stepped inside the family made him feel at home. There was a grey-haired husband, who showed signs of being a hard worker, his busy wife, two daughters - one sixteen years of age and the other twenty-five - and finally a ten-year-old son who went to a neighbour to learn carpentry skills. They seemed to be a close family.

By day, Luckas helped the man around the house, for there were several places in need of repair. At night, the family sat together at the table, and while eating they spoke about all that had happened during the day.

Luckas didn't like to interrupt the family's conversation, but the father was intrigued by this young man who had been placed into their lives and wanted to discover more about him.

"Why do you want to build a boat?" the father asked.

"I want to return to my father's castle, and sailing will be the easiest way."

"So, you are a prince?"

"Yes, sir."

They all laughed when he said he was a prince. Luckas was now beginning to wonder if anyone would ever believe him.

Luckas was told that he had to go every morning to the king's adviser to receive orders. In the beginning he was given work to cultivate the land for the king. It was hard, but he proved he could do any task that was given to him.

In the afternoons, Luckas was free to build his boat. This didn't happen right away, because the materials failed to arrive. During that time, Luckas began to wonder whether the king was going to keep his promise.

One afternoon, Luckas decided he would try to speak again with the king, but without the required permission, the sentries posted outside the tall, wooden door that led into the throne room didn't allow him access.

"Luckas," said the king's adviser, who appeared at that moment. "We have told you that the king is busy and will not speak with anyone."

"That is all I have heard for the last three weeks, but I am not receiving the materials that the king promised."

"Did the king promise?"

"He did."

"In that case, wait a little bit longer."

Just then, as Luckas was becoming impatient, Abigail appeared.

"Luckas!" she was happy to see him. "How is the boat coming on?"

"Not good! The materials have not arrived, and there is no way that I can speak to your father."

"You go back to what you were doing. I will see what I can do."

Luckas nodded, thanked her and returned to the house by the sea.

Two months went by and still there was no sign of any change. Just when Luckas was about to make another visit to the king, he couldn't believe his eyes. There were some of the king's soldiers by the sea. Among them was Abigail, with some of the materials he needed. He was overjoyed and ran with excitement towards them.

"Thank you!" Luckas ran past the soldiers and grabbed Abigail's shoulders. "Thank you so, so much."

The soldiers knew Luckas from all the times he had been to the castle, but even so, they watched every one of his moves in case he tried to harm the princess. But she was joining in with the excitement.

"I told you to be patient," she cried. "My father is a man of honour. He takes his time, but he fulfils his promises."

"Thank you," Luckas said again, giving Abigail a kiss on her cheek. Then he ran past her to the materials lying on the sand. He wanted to start work on the boat without any further delay.

Luckas had built many boats before, so he didn't need a plan. Within seconds he had started hammering in the nails to join the pieces of wood together. Abigail, meanwhile, headed back to the castle escorted by her personal guards, but only after staring at Luckas in amazement at his skills.

After receiving the materials Luckas worked on his boat from the afternoon until sunset, when there was no longer any daylight for him to continue. It was hard work without help, but in time and with patience the boat began to take shape. And because he was making good progress, he allowed himself to rest some afternoons under the shade of a tree.

Abigail visited Luckas from time to time, though she never went alone. She was always accompanied by her maidservant and five soldiers, who watched their every move. During these visits, Luckas would take a short break and walk with Abigail along the seashore, her maidservant just behind them. Luckas liked Abigail, but he knew that while he was looked upon as a villager he could only be treated as a friend. Her father wouldn't allow anything else.

As the months hurried by, the boat was now half finished. One day the king appeared with several soldiers. The king stood next to Luckas and marvelled at the vessel. He had heard of the good work that the young man had done in the fields and with his boat, so he went to make him an offer.

"Your boat," he said. "I am impressed."

"Thank you, my lord."

"However, its size tells me that it is going to need more than one man to sail it," the king added.

"I will manage, sire."

"I don't think you will finish the boat in the final three months of this year. Why not work another year for me? In exchange, I will give you two men who will help you on your journey."

Luckas looked at the boat and scratched his head. *Some help would be very handy.* But then he stared at the ocean. *Another year?*

In the end he decided to agree, not because he needed help to sail the boat, but because he wanted more time with Abigail.

21

During the mornings, Luckas carried on labouring in the fields. He became familiar with their northern ways of working, but he also improved them by combining some agricultural methods he had learnt when he ruled his fortress. To water the crops in the fields, he created several canals which guided the water from a nearby river. Wherever he worked, the crop multiplied, making the king happy with his service.

During the afternoons he continued with his boat, hammering the wooden beams that were still waiting to be positioned. Considering he was on his own, he was progressing at a good speed. He had established when he would finish the job. All the while he was motivated by the prospect of seeing his family again, for he had now forgiven those who had wronged him.

On a day when the king required him to look after his horses, Luckas and Abigail went walking around one of the royal gardens, but as usual Abigail's maidservant wasn't too far from them. It was not easy to speak openly while being observed, so that day Luckas decided to take a risk.

"Abigail," whispered Luckas.

"Yes?" she whispered back.

"Run!" He grabbed her hand and they both ran as fast as they could. Abigail's maidservant tried to follow but was having difficulty catching up with them. "Stop!" she cried.

They both laughed as they entered the woods, where they managed to lose their pursuer.

"We have made it!" Luckas was excited.

"It will not be for long."

"We will run again then."

Now alone, Luckas put his arms around Abigail and embraced her. Everything around them went quiet, and time itself seemed to stand still. The wind stopped blowing through the branches, the birds stopped singing, and the squirrels stopped running along the branches of the trees. It seemed as if the whole world was on tiptoe, watching with silent awe.

Abigail moved her hand and touched Luckas' shoulder. This caused her momentarily to remember his wound. This made her think about what she was doing. She had fallen in love with a villager. She knew that her father wouldn't allow this and with that thought she pushed Luckas away.

"This is not possible," she moaned, as tears fell down her cheeks.

"What do you mean?"

Abigail didn't answer. She just ran from Luckas. He called for her to come back, but she was gone.

Several moments later, the maidservant appeared puffing and panting out of the bushes.

"I am going after her," Luckas said.

"No, you're not," she said, her face flushed. "Abigail has told me to tell you, that she doesn't want to see you anymore."

Luckas was speechless. His heart was broken into a thousand pieces. Defeated and dejected, he turned around and began the walk home.

From then on, Luckas just wanted to be alone. Even his food lost its savour. One day, sitting on his bed, he looked through the window and saw his boat. There was still a little more work to be done and now, with Abigail's decision, there was no point in delaying any longer.

It was time to finish the boat and leave.

22

The second year flew by, and with nothing else to distract him, Luckas had finished his boat sooner than expected. He had kept himself very busy, pushing to the back of his mind thoughts of the woman he loved. But even hard work couldn't altogether blot out the memory of her.

Finally, the day Luckas had set for his departure arrived. The king and his sons came to see him off, along with many villagers, some of whom had become his friends, a few of whom tried to persuade him to stay. Everyone was there except Abigail. It was time to leave.

The boat had been built close to the seashore and required just a push to slide it into the water. It was a medium-sized vessel with a wide body, and around the border of the deck there was a handrail to prevent men from falling into the water. On the deck there was an open space which led to the interior of the boat, where the food and the hammocks were located. At the stern of the boat, two steps led to a raised platform where the wheel for the rudder was situated. The barrels and the ropes were at the bow of the boat. In the centre, was the mast with the mainsail, its tied canvas trembling in the breeze.

Whilst Luckas moved the last supplies into the ship, a group of soldiers were making a way for the king and his sons, directing the people away from their path to the boat.

"I see you are all set," the king said.

"Yes sir."

"You have laboured well, and as I promised, here are the two men who will accompany you."

"Thank you, my lord. I will send them to you as soon as we arrive at our destination."

The two men weren't given any time to relax. It was straight to work for them. Luckas, meanwhile, made the final preparations for sailing.

When everything was ready, he and his two companions pushed the boat into the ocean with the help of some of the villagers, and once in the water, they set sail to make use of the light wind. The villagers waved goodbye to their friend, cheering and shouting as they left.

From a distance, through the window of her room, Abigail watched all this in despair. It was as if a thorn had pierced her heart.

"Don't cry my dear," her mother said as she placed her hands on her daughter's shoulders.

"Why not, mother? The man I love is gone forever."

"If he is who he says he is ... he will return."

"How can you be so sure?"

"Just trust me," the mother replied.

But Abigail's eyes were misty with tears and the boat was now shrinking in the distance.

23

Once at sea, they headed west and followed the coastline on their left side. In some parts close to the coast, pointed rocks peeped out from beneath the waves, causing them to move further away from the fine golden sand along the shoreline.

The wind had been in their favour for most of the journey, and by the look of the clear blue sky it seemed that it would continue that way. A gentle breeze made their progress even more agreeable, removing the excess heat as they worked on deck.

The men had split the work in order not to become weary. When one steered the boat at a safe distance from the rocks, another worked close to the sails, ensuring that they were tight enough to make use of the wind. The third man rested and waited until it was his time to work. When it was time to eat, his job was to put his imagination to good use and provide a meal with the ingredients that they had inside the barrels.

The scenery had been constant during the journey - a vast, clear and calm ocean to their right, and a golden coast with green patches to their left. After sailing for three days, they saw the corner of the coast and manoeuvred the boat to the left, crossing over the small line of waves caused by the merging of the ocean with the sea, and entering what would be the last leg of their journey.

"Not far to go from here," Luckas said.

He was excited, but at the same time cautious. He had sailed many times through those waters and knew that at this time of the year the weather could turn without warning. This happened when the cold air rushed down from the hills and collided with the warm air, generating violent storms.

"How long have we got left?" asked one of the men.

"Just a little over a day's journey, but..." Luckas stopped and thought of how to give the bad news.

"But what?"

"We might hit very bad weather."

"You are joking, right? Look at this blue sky!"

Luckas knew that the weather couldn't be predicted by the blue sky, but by the direction of the wind. He had accordingly placed a dark blue flag on the top of the mast to keep him alert. Just as he looked up to check it, he could see how the flag had just stopped waving for a few seconds before it changed direction.

"Make ready for a storm!" he shouted.

Not long after that the wind blew harder, bringing with it thick and heavy clouds which covered the entire sky. As soon as these were on top of them, it started to rain. Each drop crashed against the wood of the boat, but that was as nothing, just the light prelude to a deafening thunderstorm as the heavens opened and hard rain began to pummel the deck. A warm and relaxing day had turned into a day of great danger in the twinkling of an eye.

"Quick! Collect the sail!" shouted Luckas.

As the waves crashed in fury against the ship, it lurched from side to side, causing them to drift towards the coast. To avoid crashing against the rocks, Luckas tried to steer the ship in the opposite direction. Having difficulty manoeuvring the wheel, one of the men went to assist him. Between the two of them they just managed to steer the boat away from the rocks.

For a moment, it seemed that they had the ship under control, but this all changed when a big wave caught the men by surprise and smashed upon the deck, dragging with it the man who had gone to tie the sail. He tried to hold onto anything he could, fearing that he was about to be pulled into the raging sea. As luck would have it, he made it to the edge of the boat and grasped the handrail for dear life.

"Help! Help me!" The man cried as his grip began to loosen.

"Hold on!" Luckas cried.

Luckas ran as fast as he could while he somehow kept his balance on the undulating deck. Just as the man's fingertips slipped and he started to fall into the sea, Luckas grasped his arm and pulled him back up on deck.

This wrestling with severe weather continued until night, when everything went dark. The boat now only illuminated by candles protected by a lamp hanging from the mast, giving some light to see what was happening on deck. Beyond deck, nothing could be seen, but that didn't mean that nothing was happening, for they could hear the roaring sound of the waves colliding without mercy against the hull of the boat. What they didn't notice was how one of the sail ropes, which they had forgotten to tighten, came loose, causing the sail to open. The men were now alarmed, not just because the wind was blowing the sail in the opposite direction to which they wanted to go, but also because the open sail was causing a significant amount of stress on the mast.

"Quick!" Luckas cried. "Cut the ropes!"

But it was too late.

The mast couldn't bear the stress any longer. With a loud crack, it snapped and fell onto the deck, causing the men to scurry for cover. Luckas jumped down the stairs and went into the interior of the boat while one of the men ran and hid on deck. The other man was paralysed with fear and stood where he was as the great beam landed with a thud just inches away from him.

When the storm at last ended, the heavy grey clouds disappeared, leaving a sparkling dotted sky. The men were exhausted, so they lay down wherever they could and fell into a deep sleep. All the while, their battered vessel floated away on a gentle current.

The following morning, Luckas' vessel arrived at one of Norandia's control points, near the fortress. Two ships had spotted it from a distance and waited, having on each deck ten archers with their bows and arrows ready. Their shouts woke the three men, who looked over the handrail to find many arrows pointing at them. Luckas wasn't surprised; he was the one who had established these security procedures in the first place. Everything was familiar to him. The guards' uniforms were the same design and colour - black loose trousers and a light blue baggy shirt, covered by a brown leather waistcoat - colours associated with this part of the kingdom. This was light uniform, designed to ensure that the wearers could still swim if they fell into the water.

"Hold fast!" said the commander. "If you want to go any further, you must show me the official papers."

"We do not have any!" shouted one of the men before Luckas could even speak.

Luckas turned and looked angrily at the man. Without any authorisation, the guards wouldn't allow anyone to continue through those waters.

"In that case, you must turn back."

"I am Luckas, son of king Staffan!"

Disturbed by what the young man had said, the guards started quarrelling, for they had been informed that Luckas had died three years ago.

"Luckas is dead!"

"I am Luckas. Take me to the king and I will prove it."

"Show me your medallion."

Luckas wished they hadn't demanded to see the medallion; he had no idea where it was.

"It fell in the sea!" Luckas said.

"You are an imposter!" The commander shouted, giving a sign to the archers.

"Luckas," said one of the men who was with him. "My king has told me to help you, but not to die for you."

"Wait!" Luckas raised his arms.

Luckas knew that they would kill him and his companions if they didn't turn back, so he had to do something as soon as possible. The archers were now primed to shoot once their leader gave the signal. Luckas scanned their faces and, as he did, he managed to recognise some of them.

"I have a way to prove to you that I am who I say I am."

"Speak. You have one last chance."

"I will tell you things about some of you, things that only Luckas would know. I will start with you," he said as he pointed at one of the archers. "You were around fifteen years old when Maryann kissed you, and your name is Reuben."

Reuben's silence said it all, as did his friends' laughter. The long-kept secret had come to light – he kissed her, not because he took the first step, but because she had forced him to.

"Your name is Symon," Luckas pointed out to another guard. "You wanted to marry Ruth. I don't know whether you did, because I haven't been around since your betrothal."

A look of astonishment spread across his face, and the commander's, to whom Luckas now turned.

"Sir, it was a rainy day when you were named commander of your ship, and two days later your wife gave birth to a son whom you named after me... Lukian. Your name is Phelps, and to start with, one of your tasks was to take care of my horses in the barn. From there you were transferred to the docks, where you continued to show diligence and faithfulness, and where after training you became commander of the ships. I know about your son's name because you asked me for my permission when the child was born."

With that, the commander knew that the young man in front of him was the prince dressed in villagers' clothes. He knelt and said nothing, bowing his head in respect. The rest observed and followed suit, realizing that the king's son was back from the dead. The two men who were with Luckas looked at him with their mouths wide open in amazement.

"You ...you ...you are a prince after all!"

Luckas didn't count that question worthy of an answer. He turned to the commander. "Now please, can you take me to my father?"

"Sir," said the commander. "Even if we escort you, we might not arrive on time."

"On time for what?"

"The investiture."

"Who has been named the king's successor?" Luckas asked.

"Your brother, Benjamen."

"That cannot be! We must stop it!"

To hasten his journey, Luckas jumped from his damaged galley onto the commander's ship, where everyone patted the young man's back, checking that he wasn't a ghost or a vision. Once all were aboard, the ship sailed at full speed, with all hands pulling at the oars. Luckas had always treated these men well. Now it was their turn to return the favour.

When the ship drew nearer to shore, one of the guards waved a white flag with a thick red line across the centre. This warning sign meant that several horses had to be prepared, for there was a messenger with an urgent message which had to be delivered to the king.

When they arrived at the harbour, some soldiers were already waiting for them with the horses which had been brought from nearby stables. Curious about all the shouting from the agitated soldiers, some local villagers stopped and observed what was happening, trying to hear if they could find out anything about the mysterious man who was being escorted from the ship to the horses.

Without any words, Luckas and his escort galloped at full speed to try to reach the castle on time. The journey to the castle was going to be long, and they couldn't allow themselves to be interrupted by any obstacle on the way. To avoid any disruptions, six soldiers on their horses had already left, leading the group and opening the way for those coming behind. Following them and not too far away, was the small group formed by Luckas and another six soldiers who protected his exposed flanks.

The king and the queen sat and watched as their son Benjamen walked through the doors to the sound of the trumpets. Soon he wouldn't be considered a young prince anymore, but the future king of Norandia. Markus and Jakob were waiting on the front bench, and next to them were his two sisters, Shanna and Rebekah, along with her husband. Seated behind them were several kings with their wives from nearby kingdoms, for Benjamen would soon have to start dealing with them. Behind those benches, there were lords and ladies from the surrounding villages. Numerous guards secured the inside of the hall and were posted at every door, window and column.

On the way to the castle, the first group of soldiers ran into a cart with its axle snapped. It was in the middle of the path, and its owner had been trying in vain to fix it. Three soldiers dismounted and helped him to move the cart to one side, while the other three continued galloping on their way to the castle. Not long after the cart was removed, the group of soldiers escorting Luckas appeared and passed them at full speed.

Back at the castle, the music had stopped, and the people were listening to what the priest had to say to the future crown prince who was standing in front of the king and queen. The prince was restless; he wanted to skip all the talking and was not taking any notice of what the priest was saying.

Time was running out for Luckas, and he didn't know if he was going to make it on time. Just when he was in danger of being overwhelmed by negative thoughts, a small glimmer of hope arose within him as he galloped over the last hill and saw the main doors of the castle. These doors were closed, and due to the important event that was taking place that day, they weren't going to be opened for anyone. The only thing that would persuade the king's guards would be urgent news from a messenger. These castle guards, however, would take some persuading. They weren't like regular soldiers; they wore black shirts to distinguish them from the other guards, and their armour had black patches on their breastplates, arm guards and thigh plates.

The soldiers who had been sent on ahead now arrived at the castle before the rest. They had left the port as soon as the horses were ready and therefore didn't know that Luckas was the messenger.

"Let us through!" demanded a soldier. "We bring a messenger with news of a war."

"Where is he?" one of the castle guards enquired.

"He is being escorted by some of our men not far behind us."

There was a loud screech from the hinges of the heavy doors as they were being opened, letting them know that the guards had accepted their story. At that, the soldiers headed towards the hall.

When Luckas and his escort entered the castle, the guards at the main door scanned every one of them. The main door closed with a loud bang behind them and they proceeded to the place where their three friends were waiting.

"Sir, you'd better hurry," one of the soldiers said to Luckas. "The priest is about to finish."

"What about the guards at the door?"

"That is our problem," said one of the men.

Seven soldiers walked towards the door while the other two waited with Luckas. As the men approached, those guarding the entrance stepped forward, unsheathing their swords.

"Brother," said one of the seven, for he recognized the guard as his own flesh and blood. "We bring someone of great honour in the king's eyes."

"Who is this person?" the armoured brother asked.

"Luckas, son of Staffan."

The brother looked conflicted. He knew as well as the other two guards that they would be sent to prison if they allowed anyone to enter the hall during the ceremony, but if the man was who he said he was, they might be in far greater trouble if they refused him entrance, for they knew how much the king loved his son Luckas.

After a few seconds of exchanging eye contact with each other, the soldiers stepped back, allowing Luckas and the others to pass.

In the meantime, Benjamen was now happy to see the priest leave and he knelt, waiting for his father, who had just left his throne and was walking towards him. The king waited for the priest to return, and when he did, he brought the golden crown which Benjamen would have to wear during the ceremony. Seeing that all was ready, King Staffan drew his sword.

Meanwhile, Luckas was beginning to feel anxious; he knew that stopping the ceremony could endanger his life. As the great doors opened, it was now or never. This was no time to be frozen to the spot. It was the moment to show courage, the kind of courage that the king's true successor would be expected to demonstrate.

Luckas walked up the steps that led to the entrance to the hall where the investiture was taking place.

As he walked into the chamber, the king's sword was raised, on the very point of alighting on Benjamen's shoulders, to signal to all assembled there that Benjamen had been chosen once and for all as the king's successor.

.

"Stop the ceremony!" shouted Luckas. Everyone was alarmed. Nobody had ever interrupted a ceremony and managed to live to tell the tale. They couldn't yet see who it was who had shouted the order. The light behind Luckas was too bright; all the people could see was the outline of a man.

"Who dares to stop the ceremony?!" The king placed the sword back in his sheath.

"I do, Father!"

The king froze. Although he couldn't see Luckas, he recognised his voice. Everyone could see that the king's hands were now shaking.

"Luckas?" Rebekah stood up as soon as she heard the voice.

The murmurs in the chamber grew louder.

"Father," Benjamen cried. "Do not forget about me. Just a little tapping of your sword here and there, and it will be finished."

"Wait," the king said.

Luckas could now see Shanna staring and squinting at him, blinded by the light pouring through the doors behind him. When she heard his voice, her eyes opened wide in disbelief. Then joy broke across her face and, without a second thought, she ran and hugged him as tears ran down her cheeks.

"I have missed you, Luckas."

"I have missed you too my little sister."

Luckas' father was finding it hard to assimilate what was going on; he had lost all hope of seeing his son alive. Now that he was in front of him, he couldn't seem to understand what was happening.

The king walked towards Luckas and the entire chamber fell silent. He stretched out his hand to touch his son's face, making sure that it wasn't a vision. It was indeed flesh he was touching. His son was real. Luckas was alive.

"You were dead," Staffan muttered.

"Is that what they told you?"

This was not the time for the king to ask his son to explain. It was the time for hugs and tears. King Staffan threw his arms around his long-lost son's shoulders, weeping with joy.

Ysabel followed a few steps behind her husband, crying out as she saw the face of the boy she thought was dead.

After that, the knights approached their lost prince with delight. Seff was among them, a little sad as well as glad – sad that he had not been able to find Luckas three years ago.

"Luckas," he said softly. "I searched for you and I could not find you. I am sorry."

"Do not worry," he said. "I am here now." Luckas smiled and stretched out his hand to grab the knight by his shoulder.

All this time, Luckas' three brothers were looking at each other in astonishment. Benjamen and Jakob looked angry, but Markus was pleased to see his brother, for he still loved him and was sorry for what he had done.

So as not to raise any suspicions, the three brothers headed towards Luckas. Benjamen and Jakob acted as if they were overjoyed, hugging Luckas as if they had missed him. Markus' tears, on the other hand, were genuine.

"Luckas, I am sorry."

"Come here." Luckas stretched his arms to hug him.

Markus couldn't believe his ears; his brother wasn't reproaching him for what had happened. Overwhelmed, he returned the embrace.

The king ruled that the investiture should be stopped and postponed for another time. "It's more appropriate to celebrate the return of my son," he decreed. "Let there be a great feast. Let the whole kingdom celebrate."

And that is what they did.

For the first few days after his arrival, Luckas spent most of his time with his family, discovering what had happened in his absence. They, in turn, came to learn about the painful things he had endured in the north.

During these days, Luckas received many visitors. They provided something of the warmth and love he had missed for so long. The only people who never thought to see him were his three brothers, one of whom stayed away because he regretted what he had done. Even though Luckas had forgiven him, he was still ashamed of it. The other two brothers were annoyed by Luckas' return and were now planning to dispose of him once and for all.

"You know our father might very well give him the crown," Jakob said.

"Yes, that is why I have arranged a meeting with a friend of mine," Benjamen replied. "With his help, we will soon know what to do."

"Who is this friend of yours?"

"It is better that you don't know, brother."

Even though Luckas was at home, he sometimes woke up in the middle of the night in terror, fearing for his life. Drops of perspiration would run down his forehead, evidence of yet another nightmare. Whenever this occurred, it was difficult for him to go straight back to sleep, so he would stand close to the window and stare out at the kingdom, shrouded in darkness. At that time of the night, everything was quiet, everything still, except for the night-watchmen on duty in the streets, carrying their flickering torches.

For Shanna, the supposed death of Luckas had been traumatic. As sister and brother, they had formed a close bond. When he returned, she was so glad to see him that she rarely left his side, enjoying taking him his breakfast and walking with him in the fields.

One day at midday, a messenger came to Luckas in his room. He had a message from the king. The messenger was a trustworthy man, so the prince didn't doubt the authenticity of the message.

"My prince, your father is in his barn. He is waiting for you."

"Did the king say anything else?"

"Just that it is urgent."

The messenger said no more and left hot footed, leaving Luckas puzzled by what could be so important. One thing he did know was that it wasn't good to keep his father waiting, so he hurried to the barn. As he was making his way through the castle, he had a sense that someone was observing him. This sense was confirmed when, through the corner of his eye he saw a shadow which disappeared as soon as he turned around. Whoever it was, they didn't want to be seen. Luckas decided not to find out who it was, especially after Seff had told him that many of his brothers' sympathizers weren't happy about his return, so he carried on walking.

There was as much mystery ahead of him as there was behind, for when Luckas arrived at the barn he found his father dressed and disguised as a villager not as a king. Luckas too was told to put on villagers' clothes.

"We are going somewhere we will not be recognised or disturbed," his father said. Just that. No more.

The two men mounted their horses and rode through fields warmed by the sunshine and beneath branches waving in the breeze. When they reached a thick copse on top of a small hill, they dismounted, tied their horses to the branches of a tree, and sat together side by side, their backs leaning against the trunk.

"Luckas, you returned at exactly the right moment. You know that don't you?"

Luckas turned and looked at his father. This close, he could see that he had more wrinkles on his brow than he remembered, and more grey flecks of hair. The three years had left their mark on his father.

"Your brother only uses the kingdom's resources for his parties," he said.

"So, I have heard."

"Our ancestors fought and worked very hard to make Norandia what it is today, which is why you have to be the successor to the throne." Staffan paused to observe his son's reaction.

"Have you told Benjamen this?" Luckas asked.

"Not yet. He still thinks that the investiture is going to go ahead. He needs to keep thinking that until the right moment arrives."

"You know he will be furious."

"He will have to accept it. If he wants to be a king one day, he must learn to be ruled before he can ever be ready to rule." Luckas could see his father's fists clenching so tight that his knuckles turned white.

"I'm confused, father. I was not the first one to be born. How can I be elevated above my brother?"

"The Law of Succession says that a younger son can only take the throne if all the other sons in line have died. Or..." the king paused and looked straight into his son's eyes. "Or if the youngest son marries before the oldest son does. Then I can overrule the Law of the Firstborn. So, what do you say, my son?"

"Father, it would be an honour."

"In that case, we will have to search for a wife for you." Staffan tapped his nose and winked at Luckas. "I have some princesses in mind…"

"Father!"

"We can go through them together and then arrange a few meetings." Staffan was now so excited that he hadn't noticed his son's reaction.

"Father!"

"A princess should be caring, supportive, and love the people," the king said, a broad smile on his face.

"Father! Wait!"

Staffan stopped, aroused from his daydreaming by the unfamiliar sound of his son's raised voice.

"I am sorry for shouting," Luckas said. "I was trying to tell you that my heart is already set on a pretty princess from the northern territories."

"The northern territories? Which one of the four kingdoms does she belong to?"

"Zophrandia, and there are only three kingdoms now. Her father conquered one of them."

"Oh, yes. I have heard that he is very ambitious."

"Yes," Luckas agreed, "but behind his hard exterior there is a soft and tender heart."

"What is her name?"

"Abigail."

"Well, then, you must tell her that you will be named my successor, and that you wish her to be your wife before that happens. Shall we arrange for the wedding to take place next spring?"

"Next spring?" Luckas' eyes opened wide.

"Well, do you love her or not?" asked Staffan. "And what about her? Does she love you?"

"Yes, she does." Luckas was blushing as he replied.

Staffan placed his right hand on his son's right shoulder, making sure he had eye contact with him. "Son, something I have learnt in life is that love never fails, never quits, never surrenders. Love is like a fire, and for it to continue burning, you will both have to do your part by stoking it, otherwise it will diminish and with time fade away. But if both of you fan the flames, it will last forever."

"Thank you, father."

Staffan stood and walked to his horse. Luckas followed. As they mounted and sat side by side, Luckas asked, "When will I be named your successor?"

"You first need to marry," Staffan replied. "And I need to keep your hot-headed brothers on a tight rein."

As they rode back through forests and meadows, Luckas remembered what had happened with Abigail before leaving Zophrandia, and for a moment he thought that she might not want to see him again, but he had to give it a try no matter what; he was still in love with her.

By the time the two men returned to the barn, the sun had set, and darkness covered their return. They resumed their normal clothes, replacing their disguises with their royal liveries. Before they rode back through the castle gates, Staffan stopped his horse. Luckas pulled up alongside him.

"My son," he said. "Leave tomorrow morning, at the crack of dawn. I have thirty soldiers who will be ready, along with provisions for the journey in a carriage. In that carriage there will be items of gold, silk garments, and silver, bejewelled platters. These are gifts for the parents of your future bride."

"Thank you, father."

"There is one more thing," the king said. "You must take with you your sister Shanna and also the two men that accompanied you on board the boat you built."

"Why Shanna?"

"Rebekah has, let's say, other duties."

"Why does Shanna need to risk coming with us?"

"It is her duty to check the suitability of the girl to whom you intend to propose. Only when she has given my blessing are you to go ahead. She knows my heart. She will tell you."

"Was that Shanna following me to the barn this morning?" Luckas asked.

The king tapped his nose again and winked.

And with that, they parted company at the stables, Luckas returning to his chambers to make ready for the journey at daybreak.

28

Many days after the group had departed, a general ran through the corridors of a great castle in the northern territories, into the throne room of King Cyrenius. "Sire," he said, recovering his breath. "I bring news."

"Continue."

"A troop of foreign soldiers has entered our kingdom."

The king, who had been leaning back into his throne, his hands resting on the golden armrests, sat upright, his hands clasped together, his eyes ablaze. "How many?" he asked.

"There are thirty soldiers. They seem to be escorting a man, a woman, and two others."

"Where are they now?"

"They have just passed through the outer perimeter. They aren't proceeding swiftly. They have a carriage that looks heavy laden."

"They may be traders, or distinguished visitors. Whatever the case, I should have been informed sooner!" The king banged the armrest with his clenched fist. "Call a meeting with my advisors."

"Very good, my lord."

"And one more thing."

"My lord?"

"Be on alert, you might have to gather some soldiers together."

"Sire."

The king was in no hurry. He needed to know for certain that this would not be the beginning of a forthcoming war, and for that, he had been speaking and discussing the matter with his officers and advisors in the council chamber until they were interrupted by his general.

"My king," his general said. "The group of soldiers is now within sight of the walls of the castle. We have counted thirty-four people in total."

"Do you think they mean harm?" the king asked, suppressing his anger at the thought of the effrontery of such a small force.

"It is impossible to say," the general replied.

"Then take me to the wall!" demanded the king.

Within minutes, the king was watching the small band approaching the gates. There was nothing in their demeanour or gait to suggest that they were intent on mischief. They looked to all intents and purposes like harmless visitors, except that whoever these visitors were, they had come heavily protected by soldiers in arms riding impressive warhorses festooned with glinting armour and colourful robes.

"What shall we do, your majesty?"

"Those soldiers look menacing," the king replied. "Prepare the king's watch to engage them."

"Shouldn't someone be sent to listen to what they have to say?"

"And give them a chance to move any closer? No!"

"Father," interrupted Davian. "Let me go disguised as a messenger, and then, when I am close enough to their leader, I will kill him."

"You are too precious to me, my son."

"I insist father! If I am to be king someday, I want to be able to earn the right to be your successor!"

The king knew he couldn't refuse. It was now a matter of honour.

As his son left, the king turned to his general. "Command the king's watch to mount their horses and tell them to be ready to attack."

Davian, disguised as a messenger, secreted several small knives in a band about his back. He galloped towards the visitors, holding with his left hand a long pole with a white flag.

When he reached the visiting party, Davian dismounted, the white flag fluttering in the wind above his head. The king observed all this from the walls, praising his son every step of the way.

A man dismounted. He and Davian were exchanging words, but at this long distance the king had no idea what they were saying.

"He will kill him any moment," the king said. "You mark my words."

But then something unexpected happened. His son turned back towards the battlements and waved at him, signalling for the soldiers to stand down and for the gates to be opened.

"Something's strange here," the king said, as he saw his son throwing his arms around the man's shoulders.

"What shall we do, my lord?" asked a general.

"Go and rescue my son!" the king said.

"Cyrenius, wait!" Salwa and Abigail now appeared. They were hurrying towards him.

"Not now, my love!" the king said. He was so used to this. Cyrenius, truth to be told, enjoyed fighting. It was like a game to him, but whenever he wanted to attack an enemy, his wife would turn up and try to give him a better, less violent solution. He loved his wife, so he listened to her advice, but sometimes he took it and other times he didn't.

"Father, please wait," Abigail cried. "I think I recognise him. It's ..."

"Do not mention that name!" the king shouted. "He went and he is gone! General ..." The king was about to issue the order to attack.

"Father, please!"

"Cyrenius! We have talked about this!" Salwa raised her voice.

Salwa had a strong personality, and if she wanted something done her way she was determined to make her case heard. This was a quality that attracted Cyrenius to her.

"Let them at least come closer," Salwa said. "Then we will be able to see who they are."

The king reluctantly relented.

As the group drew nearer and their faces became more visible, the king couldn't believe his eyes. The villager who had left in a boat had arrived surrounded by an escort fit for a prince.

"Maybe that young man was telling the truth after all," he muttered.

"It is Luckas!" Salwa cried.

"But who is that lady with him?" Abigail said, her voice trailing, her hopes dying. "Has he come to introduce me to his bride?"

"Now, now, daughter," the king said. "Don't jump to conclusions. It could be anyone. Believe the best."

The king gave a further order and the visitors entered the castle, finding themselves confronted by a company of horsemen who had been ready a moment earlier to attack and kill them. Instead, they were now lowering their weapons and moving to one side, allowing the visitors to pass through the courtyard and through another gate into the vast grounds beyond.

Several minutes later, the king arrived with some pomp, accompanied by a fanfare of trumpets.

"Luckas!" Cyrenius bellowed "I have to admit that you have surprised me. I never thought you were telling the truth about being a prince. Forgive me. That was most discourteous."

"You had no reason to believe me," Luckas replied.

"And who is this fine-looking young lady?" the king asked.

"Now it is my turn to ask your forgiveness," Luckas said. "Please excuse my terrible manners. This is my sister Shanna."

With that, there was a squeal of delight from behind the king and Abigail appeared, smiling from ear to ear, her eyes sparkling with love. The next moment, she and Luckas, who had dismounted his horse, were running into each other's arms, embracing, kissing, laughing.

"King Cyrenius," Luckas said when he had calmed down. Abigail was standing next to him, her hand clasping his. "I have come to ask for your daughter's hand in marriage."

"Oh!" the king exclaimed. "I see."

The king looked at his daughter's face, flushed with love, radiant with life. There was no doubting her affections for this southern prince, and he had more than proved his worth in the two years he had spent in his kingdom. So, knowing his decision already, the king decided to have a little game.

"Well, I had planned for her to marry someone else. Her portly cousin Garton, whose clothes reek of the pigs he keeps."

"Father!" Abigail screamed. "Don't jest!"

The king roared with laughter, and in truth, the soldiers with him could barely keep the grins from their faces and were even now stifling their laughter. One of them failed to stop a giggle.

"What's that?" the king stormed, feigning rage.

"Nothing, my lord," the poor soldier stammered, his face suddenly a pale green colour, as if he was about to wretch.

"What say you, my queen?" the king asked, turning to Salwa.

"I say yes," she answered.

"As do I!" the king declared.

There was a cheer from the growing crowd.

"How long will you and your men stay?" the king asked.

"One week," Luckas replied. "Two weeks at the most, if it is fine with you."

"Of course, it is! Tomorrow morning, after you have all had some of our best wine, finest victuals and a good rest, we will share gifts with each other. In the meantime, you and my daughter have a lot of catching up to do and we would like to get to know your sister."

The king looked at Abigail, her eyes shining as if the sun had emerged from behind dark clouds. "And tomorrow morning," he said, "we all have a wedding to prepare!"

The following morning, after Luckas had presented the gifts of his kingdom to his hosts, Cyrenius, escorted by fifteen of his personal guards, took Luckas beyond the castle walls. Seff, who had accompanied Luckas disguised as a humble soldier, went with the prince as his bodyguard.

"Where are we going?" Luckas asked.

"It's a secret," the king replied.

They headed north for over an hour, arriving at what seemed to be dense woodland. To continue their journey, they had to go deep into the forest, where the wide tall trees had thick canopies which only allowed glimpses of the sunlight, enough to allow the men to see where they were going. It seemed as if the horses knew where they were supposed to stop, for they came to a sudden halt, and the king dismounted.

"Luckas, you come with me. The rest of you stay here."

"It's all right," Luckas said, turning to Seff. "You stay with the others. We are perfectly safe."

Cyrenius and Luckas carried on by foot and disappeared. Soon Luckas saw a reddish glow ahead. On closer inspection, he realised that he was looking at a flickering fire. It was visible to their eyes, but invisible to anyone outside the woods. *This truly is a secret place,* the prince thought.

As Luckas continued to scrutinize his surroundings, he saw how the trees had grown right to the water's edge. The water from what appeared to be an ocean was lapping at their roots.

"Luckas, I saw you duelling with my son last time you were here, and I have to admit that you are a strong fighter. So, as a wedding gift I want to give you a sword, which is what a warrior deserves."

Luckas already had a sword waiting for him at home, so he looked at the king wondering what was so special about this one. However, despising a king's gift would be the worst insult, so he accepted it with gratitude.

"It is a sword which has been forged by the elders in the deepest part of the forest, and it has been cooled down with the water of the ocean, making it one of the strongest metals. I believe we will face difficult times soon, and I think you might need a sword like this."

They stopped at the entrance of a tent. Just then, an old man, clothed in an olive-green tabard, came out of the tent with a sword and handed it with great gravitas to Cyrenius, who in turn passed it to Luckas. Luckas couldn't believe how light it was, nor how ornately it had been decorated. His name was inscribed in finely carved letters on the metal hilt.

"Thank you," Luckas bowed his head.

Then a familiar face emerged from the tent, Salwa's. She too was dressed in olive-green, the colour of the woods, and a dark brown cape. She was wearing what seemed a very strange crown, whose silver sides were intertwined with the carvings of small twigs and branches, painted green and brown, making her look like a noble creature of the forest. She was carrying a green velvet cushion, with a tiny chest on it, smaller than her fist.

The queen spoke. "One of the precious stones of our kingdom," she said, bearing the gift to Luckas. "For my future son-in-law. May it be a symbol of peace between our kingdoms."

Luckas bowed and took the treasure chest, placing it on the palm of his left hand. With his right hand he opened it. A golden light seemed to shine from within. As the prince adjusted his focus, he saw that it was an emerald stone, the largest he had ever seen. The green mineral seemed to the prince's eyes to be deeper than the deepest oceans and his heart was filled with wonder.

"This stone has a special quality," the queen said. "If it is kept in the dark, it will appear to be an ordinary dark green colour, but when it is left outside in the sun, a green light will shine in all directions. It will absorb the sunbeams in the daytime, and it will emit the light in a supernatural way during the night."

"I cannot thank you enough," Luckas said.

Bearing both his gifts, the sword and the stone, Luckas returned with the king and his queen to their horses and returned with their escort to the castle. Seff drew alongside his prince on the way. "How did it go?" he asked.

"I have a new sword," Luckas replied. "And an emerald stone. The sword is a fine blade, inscribed with my name. The stone, well, it is strange."

"In what way?"

"It seems to have unusual powers."

Luckas made it clear that this was as much as he wanted to say, and so Seff moved behind his master and followed him back to the castle.

For the next three days, Luckas spoke about the wedding with the king and queen. As there were clear blue skies and plenty of sunshine, they spent some of the time outside, even enjoying a picnic or two.

It was on one occasion, when Luckas went for a walk with Seff that Abigail appeared. She was wearing a dark blue, full-length silky dress, which matched the colour of her eyes. She had not spent any time with Luckas, due to the long discussions about the wedding preparations and other matters of state.

"I will leave you two so that you can talk," Seff said. "I will not be too far away, if you need me."

As soon as Seff had disappeared, Abigail melted in his arms.

"Luckas," she sighed. "It has been horrible not being able to be with you like this. Do you really want to marry me?"

Luckas didn't say a word. He took hold of her chin and kissed her on the lips, gently, tenderly, slowly. In that moment, all her doubts lifted from her like butterflies on the wind. That single kiss was enough for both to return to Seff with a new brightness in their soul and a new lightness in their steps. They were in love. That was certain. And they were going to be married the following spring. That was now certain too.

And so, the time accelerated, as it always does for those in love, and within what seemed like no time at all, two weeks had passed, and it was now time for the prince and his entourage to return to Norandia. Shanna and Abigail had become firm friends and their farewell was a tearful one, but not as tearful as that between the prince and his future bride. They lingered in each other's arms, wishing the months away, desperate for the leaves to reappear on the trees and life to be restored to the earth. Abigail soaked her prince's epaulettes with her sobbing. He, in turn, buried his nose in her long hair, relishing her fragrance as if it was the last breath of his life.

"Until the Spring!" The king decreed.

As they rode away, the prince's sister drew alongside her bother.

"Luckas?"

"Yes, Shanna."

"You have made the right decision."

"Do you think so?"

"Without any doubt."

"Why?"

"She is kind, warm-hearted, and very beautiful."

"She is, isn't she?" said the prince, a smile spreading across his heart like the first dawn of a new Spring.

The first day of Spring was greeted by a myriad of flowers, covering the fields with a yellow, orange, red and purple throw. These vivid hues awakened and cheered the people, along with the sense of excitement in the air. Everyone was speaking about it; the King's son was to be married that very day.

To mark this, all the villages had been decorated with blue and white banners which were now hanging over the cobbled streets. Outside each village, in open spaces, small fires were being lit to roast the meat for the feast. Scorching flames were licking at the hogs, slow cooking their flesh on a hand-rotated spit. These beasts had been given as a gift by the king. The several villagers tasked with the responsibility of preparing each hog were timing the process carefully; the meat had to be ready by midday.

Along with the meat, the king had ensured early in the morning that many barrels of wine had been distributed around the villages. To hide these away from the sun, they were placed in the shade of the trees. To keep people from temptation, the king had ordered that all the wine should be guarded by his soldiers until the ceremony was over.

During the morning, some of the people went out to the fields to collect the crops, stopping at midday to join the rest of the villagers for the feast. Those who came in from the fields brought potatoes, carrots and other vegetables for the chefs to cook in large pans.

Those who weren't involved in harvesting dressed in their finest garments and went to the castle to join in with the nuptial celebrations. They weren't allowed to be present in the church because all the seats had been assigned to royal guests. This didn't deter them, however; they headed to the castle square and waited for the ceremony to end. This space was now packed with spectators longing to catch a glimpse of the married couple. Once full, the rest of the people waited along the streets and outside the walls of the castle.

Most of the elderly citizens stayed by the roaring fires where the hogs were roasting; it was too far for them to walk, too long for them to stand. Now they were waiting, as everyone else in the kingdom was, for all the bells of every church to chime at the same time, signalling that the ceremony was complete and that the knot had been tied.

Throughout these first hours of the day, great crowds of people were travelling on all the pathways leading to the castle. To make sure that there was a continuous flow of traffic, sentries were placed in pairs at regular intervals along each route, tasked to keep things moving.

To protect the kingdom from opportunistic enemy incursions into the kingdom, companies of armed soldiers reinforced all the entrances to Norandia. Only those who had been invited to the wedding were given access. The sea was also patrolled by ships, and only those invited to the wedding docked in the port.

The king was aware that a minority wanted his son Benjamen to be king. To ensure that these people didn't spoil the great day, soldiers kept watch on the rooftop of the church and in the turrets of the castle, using the high ground as observation posts.

As the morning wore on, royal carriages, dragged by strong and well-fed horses, began to stop at the front of the church and guests began to alight and enter the sacred building. Once their load had been lightened, the coachmen took the carriages outside the walls of the castle, where they were ordered to wait until the end of the ceremony.

The villagers who had arrived early and managed to find a place close to the church were able to study the guests, admiring their glittering jewellery and the ornate patterns on the women's dresses. The men were clothed according to their rank, kings in regal robes and shiny crowns, landlords in stylish hats, some of which were adorned with colourful feathers.

On the steps of the church, twelve soldiers in ceremonial uniform waited in two parallel lines facing each other. Not far from them, eight soldiers guarded the door to the entrance of the church, four in the interior and four outside the heavy oak doors which had a special canopy composed of green leaves and white flowers. These doors were to stay open until midday, but as soon as the ceremony was about to start, they would be shut.

On the other side of the entrance, a scarlet carpet led all the way to the chancel. About midway there, it branched off ninety degrees to the right where it led to another door. Beside this door stood the court herald dressed in his best attire. He was holding a golden metal pole, banging it against the floor every time he announced the arrival of a royal guest. The invited kings and queens, princes and princesses, lords and ladies, were seated on scarlet cushions decorated with golden braiding. Like everyone else, they were now eager for the four chairs at the front to be filled. Every eye was upon them.

Inside the church, guards stood to attention, grasping decorated spears with both hands. Their eyes were fixed straight ahead, but if you looked closely enough, you could see how, from time to time, they would glance to check on the guests. They were monitoring every person and every movement, making sure that no one disrupted the wedding.

The sunlight was now pouring through the large stained-glass windows containing depictions of the history of Norandia, casting shafts of light on the red and white flowers which encircled the ten white columns that supported the ceiling and roof of the church.

The church choir stood on the upper floor looking down towards the chancel, out of sight of the guests. On the same level, on the right-hand side of the choir, trumpeters lifted their brass instruments. As an officer waved his hand, they released a fanfare. At that moment the whispering ceased, and the whole place became silent. The ceremony was about to begin.

The court herald knocked on the floor three times with his golden pole to proclaim the names of those about to enter. "The King and Queen of Norandia!" he announced as the doors started to open.

Everyone stood and watched Staffan and Ysabel walk towards their chairs, positioned just before the left side of the chancel. They would be sitting near the platform where the priest would lead the ceremony. Their steps were firm and calculated, not one too long nor one too short, and when they arrived, the king sat on his chair and the queen sat to his right.

Then the official knocked the floor again. "The Queen of Zophrandia!"

The trumpeters blew their trumpets once again, this time to welcome Salwa. She walked towards the chancel where she left the chair next to Staffan empty for Cyrenius, occupying the chair to the left. They sat beneath two flags, representing the two kingdoms to be united. The flag of Norandia was blue, and in its centre it had a golden eagle with its wings outstretched as it stood on a white mountain peak. Behind its large brown body there were two golden swords in a cross shape pointing downwards. Next to it was the flag of Zophrandia, divided into two colours by a diagonal line through the middle, white on the bottom left and red on the top right. In the centre, there were two orange lions with enormous manes. They stood on their back legs. With their front paws, they held a sword with a lion's head on its hilt.

After they were seated, the court herald knocked on the floor once with his golden pole, and the guests sat. Not long after that he knocked again, but this time it was four times, giving the established sign for the groom to come through the door. All the guards inside the church knocked on the floor once with the shaft of their spears, accompanying the resounding sound with a roaring shout. Now it was Luckas' turn to enter.

Luckas had been nervous in the lead up to this moment, but when the time arrived for him to walk to the altar, he managed not to exhibit his trepidations. As all eyes fixed on him, he chose to walk with noble steps. On the outside, he looked dignified and graceful. Inside, he was terrified.

Luckas was wearing a white, long-sleeved shirt, and a black linen coat and waistcoat which had golden braiding all along the edges, the neck and around the cuffs of the coat. From the top of the breast area of the coat and waistcoat to the bottom there was embroidered a fleur-de-lis with two thistles encircled by a zigzag oval. This pattern was repeated all the way down to the bottom, where his black trousers were tucked inside his black boots.

A few paces behind, there followed his groomsmen - his brother Markus on his right side and Davian on his left - and once at the altar they turned to the right to bow in reverence to the royals, after which they positioned themselves on the left side of the pulpit as they waited for the bride. When the trumpets played again, all eyes turned from Luckas to the door.

Two young flower girls in pale blue dresses walked in and headed towards the altar, throwing white and pink rose petals on the floor from their small baskets, leaving a path of flowers behind them.

And now the bride entered. Her face was covered by a veil held in place by a silver diadem with multiple small diamonds. Her auburn brown hair hung loose in curls at the back of her head, and from each side, a plait decorated with daisies formed a luscious crown braid. No one could keep their eyes off her, least of all Luckas, who was beaming with pride and affection.

Her wedding dress was made of white linen and had an open neck. On her bodice, there was a golden braided inverted triangle with golden flowers embroidered in it. The braiding continued from the bottom point of the triangle all around her waist, separating the bodice from the full skirt of the dress which continued to the floor with a train of three feet. The sleeves started with a tight fit at the shoulders, widening from the elbow down to the wrist. In her hands, she held a bouquet of white roses, blue iris, fern and three peacock feathers.

Father and daughter took steady steps, enjoying their last walk together before she was handed over to her future husband. Behind the veil you could see her smile, in contrast to Cyrenius who looked solemn and grave. He may not have looked joyful, but he was delighted for his daughter.

Following in pairs right behind them, walked eight bridesmaids dressed also in pale blue dresses. When they reached the altar, Cyrenius headed towards his seat, leaving his daughter to stand next to Luckas. They both turned and bowed in reverence before the sovereigns.

The young couple now shared nervous smiles with each other as they waited for the priest. A small squeak came from the back of the chancel, giving notice that the priest was entering, and without delay he walked towards the couple, standing in front of the pulpit where the sacred manuscripts were placed. As he arrived, an angelic hymn washed over the guests, sung by the invisible choir behind them. As soon as the choir finished, a deep silence fell inside the church, allowing the priest to start the ceremony with the words, "We have all come together in the presence of God to witness the marriage of Luckas and Abigail."

In what followed, the priest read from the sacred texts, blessing the couple in their union, calling on the assembled crowd to honour the sacred institution of marriage, asking if anyone had any just cause to object to the union. No one spoke. You could have heard a pin drop. Then the priest asked the two to turn and face each other and led them through their vows. Luckas and Abigail held each other's hands as they made their promises, staring into each other's eyes.

After the rings had been presented and given, the priest declared that they were now husband and wife. A hymn was sung, another blessing was pronounced, and with that, the whole ceremony had finished in the twinkling of an eye.

The bells now started to chime, and white and pink petals descended from above, falling upon the surprised guests. Luckas, thrilled by all that had happened, shook off his shyness and placed his arms around Abigail's waist, giving her a tender kiss. Then the young couple held hands and hurried towards the doors, which were opened by the guards.

As they walked out of the church, a representative from the royal aviary opened the door of a cage that held one hundred doves. These flew out and up over the heads of the young couple and later over the villagers until they each became a disappearing dot in the clear blue sky.

The prince and his bride waved as the crowds cheered. The more they waved, the more the people cheered. They then walked down to the bottom of the stairs where a white and open carriage was waiting for its two special passengers. Next to it, ten horsemen dressed in their ceremonial uniforms stood still. Before the couple entered the carriage, they passed under the two lines of guards who held their swords in the air. Once in the carriage, a single snap of a whip set the six white horses in motion. They pulled the carriage with ease, through the ten horsemen who had made way for them. Six knights and ten mounted soldiers escorted the carriage, following it closely.

As soon as the carriage started moving, the twelve men who had been waiting for this moment let loose the carrier pigeon they each had in a cage. The pigeons flew away to the villages where they had been trained to go. Meanwhile, the carriage took the married couple back to the castle, where rooms had been allocated for different festivities. One was for dancing. Another was for meeting relatives not seen in many years. Then there was the dining room, where succulent meats were being served, along with a selection of desserts - cakes and exotic fruits from distant lands, tempting to the eye.

Villages throughout the entire kingdom joined in the celebrations as soon as the carrier pigeons arrived. A trumpet blew to inform the villagers that the party was about to commence.

This went on for three days, and after the third day things returned to normal and the villagers went back to work.

However, the festivities didn't end there for the married couple. Another party was awaiting them in Zophrandia.

Cyrenius and Salwa accompanied Luckas and Abigail there, escorted by three knights and fifty soldiers.

The time now came for Staffan to name his successor to the crown. He knew that Benjamen should have been the one to take his place, but he was aware that if he named him king disgrace would fall upon the kingdom. He was therefore going to overrule tradition and name his youngest son, as he had met all the moral requirements to be his successor. Staffan knew what he wanted to do, but the most difficult thing was going to be explaining his decision to his sons, so he arranged a meeting with them.

It was a bright, sunny day, but before Benjamen made the journey to see his father he made sure that the torch on the external right side of his bedroom window was lit. It made no sense lighting a torch in daylight, but it was the sign that he had agreed upon to inform his friend, who would be watching from a distance, that something was about to happen.

The king's meeting was to take place in the courtroom, where the king had ordered his servants to place four seats in front of his own. The room was spacious, and it had five large windows. The main door was located to the left of the king's chair, and opposite that door there was a smaller one, which was only used by the servants of the castle. In other circumstances, there would have been one sentry posted at each door, but on this occasion Staffan had assigned two; they were ordered not to let anyone enter until he had finished.

When Benjamen entered before the others and saw that the windows were closed, he ran across to open them all. There was still one last thing he had to do; while his brothers were entering the room, he hung a piece of red cloth outside the middle window. He managed to insert the material inside a crack under the bottom frame while looking back through the corner of his eyes, making sure that his brothers weren't watching him.

Staffan entered the room with a determined look; he knew what had to be done, and it couldn't be delayed any longer. As he sat and waited for his sons to do the same, he saw Benjamen staring out of the window showing no intention of moving. "Benjamen," the king said. "Thank you for letting fresh air into the room. Now can you please sit down, as we have an important matter to discuss."

"As you wish, Father."

"I assume you all know why we are here," started Staffan.

Benjamen was the first to respond. "We have had so many meetings these last few days that I am a bit lost, so please enlighten us."

Staffan could sense a nervous tone in his son's comment. Nevertheless, he continued with the matter in hand. "I want Luckas to be my successor."

"No!" Shouted Benjamen. "You know that I am the oldest, and by right the throne belongs to me!"

"Benjamen," Staffan's tone was tender. "You have not been responsible, and it seems to me that you are not willing to change."

"Please! Give me more time and I will prove you wrong."

"I already gave you an extra year, and what reports do I receive back? Nothing but disappointing ones. You just fritter away all the money!"

"There is a reason for that. My people work hard, and, in compensation, I allow them to have parties, to keep them happy."

"Too happy. I have news that your villagers are drunk almost every day."

"Like I said, Father, I keep them happy."

Staffan was so stunned he couldn't speak.

"Father?"

"Yes Jakob," he said, turning to his other son.

"I understand why you do not want Benjamen, for I have had to raise the taxes of my villages in order to maintain the wealth of the kingdom. I am the second oldest. Why not me?"

"Jakob, you are right, but as a king you would be missing one thing, and that is love for your people. Your love of money is more important to you than the love you should have for your villagers. Yes, you have increased the taxes, but you haven't been merciful to those who couldn't pay you. You have cruelly coerced them into forced labour and treated them as slaves."

"How did you...?" Jakob stuttered before falling silent.

Staffan looked at Markus.

"Father," Markus said. "You know the way I think, and it is something that I cannot change, so I will be happy with whatever decision you make."

"Thank you, my son."

During the next two hours, Benjamen became more and more irritated and tried to convince his father to make him his successor.

Jakob was also trying to present his views, and Markus and Luckas only spoke when the rest wanted to hear what they had to say. Even though the final decision was going to be made by Staffan, he still wanted to make sure that his sons would come to some sort of agreement, so that they wouldn't fight each other and cause the kingdom to disintegrate into factions.

While they were talking, a soldier from Luckas' fortress entered the castle carrying a brown bag. He knew where to go, so without delay he asked to see the king's councillor, who at that time was busy, but one of the king's guards was happy to guide him and take him to a room where he could wait for him. The royal guard lead the soldier through narrow corridors until he was about to open the door. Before he had a chance of opening it, the soldier drove his sword into the royal guard's chest.

Without hesitating, the soldier hurried to the king's courtroom, leaving the sword behind. As he ran, he withdrew a bow and several arrows from his brown bag. He knew that if he was found wandering through the castle corridors he would be stopped, so he followed the instructions he had received to perfection, finding himself not far from the main door that gave access into the courtroom. On arrival, he spied two soldiers there; they presented no problem. He aimed with his bow and arrow and hit both men with precision, killing both.

The soldier was near to his objective and had to be quick. Sooner or later someone would find the dead bodies on the floor and everyone would be alerted. There was no time to lose.

The king was still talking to his sons when suddenly the door opened. The visitor entered unannounced and was so abrupt that it annoyed the king.

"Who dares to interrupt the king's audience?" he shouted.

The man removed a white cloth from the tip of the arrow he was about to shoot and then loosed it from his bow. Staffan tried to evade the arrow but it entered his right thigh. The king groaned in pain.

Everyone had been caught off guard, but once they realized the danger they were in, they moved fast. Markus and Jakob ran towards their father and kept guard over him. Benjamen shouted for the guards. Luckas ran towards the man at the door who was about to shoot again. When the two soldiers from the opposite door entered the room, he redirected his bow and shot two arrows at them, leaving them wounded. Seeing Luckas just feet away, he tried to run.

When Luckas reached the door, he grabbed a sword from one of the soldiers lying on the floor. Benjamen, who was following behind, opted to do the same. It seemed that the man was familiar with the castle, for he was running with a purpose, knowing where to go. Luckas followed, hoping that sooner or later he would come to a dead end. Benjamen wasn't far behind him.

It seemed that the man knew which corridors to avoid, but as they came to a crossing Luckas took a left turn. Benjamen was confused to see his brother run in a different direction from the assassin, so he stopped following his brother and went after the man.

Luckas knew the castle well and, after taking several turns and running towards the end of the corridor, he could hear some hurried footsteps. He saw the assassin and hurled himself at him, catching him by surprise and throwing him against the wall. The assassin pushed Luckas away and tried to escape, but the young prince acted fast and placed the point of his sword at the man's throat.

"Who sent you?!!"

The man looked at him but didn't say a word.

Luckas was shocked, not because the stranger wasn't answering when his life was being threatened, but because he was wearing the armour of a soldier from his own fortress.

Luckas was now confused.

A traitor from my fortress? Why?

Luckas was now losing patience. He pushed the sword tip a little further into the skin of the man's throat. A trickle of blood began to seep from the tiny wound, no more than a pin prick.

"Tell me! Who are you? Who sent you?"

By this time Benjamen had arrived and was walking towards them both, his sword drawn. Seeing him, the assassin smiled.

"Well done, brother," said Benjamen as he patted his brother's shoulder.

"My ..." the man was about to say.

"No!" shouted Luckas.

Before the man had finished his sentence, Benjamen had stabbed him in the heart. The man's eyes opened wide in shock. His smile disappeared, and he breathed his last breath, moaning as he exhaled.

"There is no mercy for traitors, brother," Benjamen muttered.

"But we could have found out who he was and who had sent him!"

"By his appearance, I would say that it is one of your soldiers."

"Impossible! There are no traitors among my men."

"That will need to be proved," Benjamen said.

With the arrival of a detachment of soldiers at the scene, the news soon spread fast and all the guards were on full alert. No one in the castle could move unless he was searched and questioned first.

Benjamen and Luckas now had only one thing on their minds. They rushed to their father's room. On entering, they saw how the doctors were trying to do everything they could to save the king's life. Nurses were hurrying in and out of the room to fetch them fresh water.

"How is Father?" asked Benjamen.

"We have removed the arrow. He would have been fine if it was not for the poison."

"Poison?"

"Yes, it appears that the tip of the arrow has been bathed in some sort of venom, and we are trying to figure out a cure for it."

"You take good care of him," Benjamen said. "We will try to find out who sent this man."

Over the following days, everyone was questioned, including Luckas and his guards and soldiers. Everyone was under scrutiny. Benjamen led the investigation, trying to find out who the intruder was and who he worked for, but no one knew him, which made the process fruitless. This incident destroyed Luckas' soldiers' reputation, and they were no longer trusted by the villagers.

In the meantime, Staffan was in agony, fighting for his life. Each day the doctors brought what they thought would be a cure for the king, and just when it seemed that his condition was stabilizing, the high fever returned. Moving was proving to be challenging, and when he did, he groaned, for his muscles were throbbing in pain.

Ahron was studying the king's symptoms and had an idea what he was fighting against. He knew there was a rare flower which could cure the king, but it could only be found on certain mountains, so he went with a group of soldiers on an expedition to find it.

After three days had passed and the doctors had tried all that they knew, all hope was gone. They couldn't find anything to help him, not even from their books, and all they could do now was wait for the moment he would die. The queen sat beside him and held his hand, knowing that her husband was going to die sooner or later.

Ahron had been away for what seemed like a long time, but when he arrived he rejoiced; he had found the flower. He rushed back to the king's room and started to prepare a liquid.

"Quick, boil about two fingers of water in this pan," commanded Ahron. He had brought a bunch of the healing flowers together with their roots, wrapped with care in a white silky cloth. The petals were of two colours; the outer leaves were purple, and the inner leaves were orange. The petals on their own could do nothing, for they had to be combined with their roots. When the water boiled, Ahron introduced the roots in the pan and left them there. In the meantime, he removed the petals and crushed them to pulp in a bowl. Then he poured the boiling water into the bowl with the mashed petals and stirred it until they both combined, forming a thick liquid texture. Finally, he mashed the roots while he waited for the liquid to cool down. The roots were harder, but he was only interested in the juice which could be extracted from them after being squashed, and this he later poured into the mixture.

Once the liquid was cool enough, he placed the bowl next to the king's mouth and made him drink. By the expression on the king's face, it must have been the bitterest thing he had ever tasted, but he didn't complain. Nothing else could be done for the king now.

After an hour had passed, the doctors noticed that the fever had disappeared. However, they were expecting it to come back at any time, just as had happened before. To their surprise the fever never came back; in fact, the moaning and complaining stopped too. It appeared that the king was recovering from his illness and so they left him alone to sleep.

When the king woke up he was amazed to hear that he had been sleeping for two days. Realizing there were many things to be done he tried to get out of bed, but he wasn't allowed to move until he had recovered. Staffan couldn't stay still, so he called his councillor, and with his help he prepared a document that stated that the king was going to transfer his power and authority to Luckas. He heard all the stories about who the traitor was and the clothes he had been wearing, but he knew deep inside that Luckas wasn't the instigator of the attempt on his life. The councilor grabbed a candle and melted red wax at the bottom of the document, where the king pressed his ring and left his stamp.

"Now hide that document until the appointed time," the king said. "Open that wardrobe and pin it inside my wife's black dress."

32

The king began to recover and was soon going to be well enough to leave his room. Before that, while he was still bedridden, he had a visitor. At that time in the afternoon, the king wasn't expecting anybody, but since his loneliness was the source of tedium for him, he welcomed the visit. Seeing that the man was of a pleasant disposition, he bid him draw closer. But the man was not what he seemed. As he stood beside the royal bed, he seized a pillow and smothered the king's face before he had a chance to cry out to the guards outside his chamber. The king was soon unconscious, his body still. To make sure he was dead, the intruder took a knife and stabbed the king in the heart.

The assassin left the room, acting normally, even nodding at the guard outside, confirming that all matters had been discussed. Not long after, the guard also walked away, leaving his post unattended.

It was Luckas who discovered the king's body. He had gone to see his father as the sun set. As he had approached the king's bed, he had noticed that the room was dark, so he lit a lamp.

"Father?" he said, seeing that the king was lying at a strange angle, his head protruding from underneath a pillow.

As Luckas lifted the light to his father's face, he knew straight away.

"Father!"

Luckas held his father in his arms. The body was cold and rigid. The dagger that had dispatched the king was still in his chest. As Luckas felt the hard hilt on his shoulder, he lowered the body to the mattress. It was then that he saw it. The dagger was his own. Someone had stolen and used it to murder the king and implicate Luckas.

As this thought struck him like a hammer blow, Benjamen entered the room and saw his brother. "What are you doing Luckas?"

"It is Father! He has been murdered!"

"Do not be foolish," Benjamen said, pushing past his brother. Seeing the king's body, he changed his tune. Observing the dagger, he shouted, "What have you done? You've killed him!"

"No."

"Your dagger says otherwise."

"But I didn't."

"Nobody will believe that."

"But what can I do?"

"You can do nothing, my brother. Nothing at all. You must run away from Norandia, as far away as you can. And you must not delay. There is not a moment to lose. The guards will be here any moment."

"What are you talking about? I would never do such a thing to Father, everyone knows that. You know that, brother. And Norandia is my home. I am not going anywhere!"

"I'm telling you, brother. You must run for your life. If you're caught now, with this evidence, you'll be hanged for high treason."

Overwhelmed by fear and confusion, panic gripped Luckas' soul like a tightening noose. The only thing he knew was that his brother was right. Although he was innocent, he looked guilty. He opened the door and ran, bumping into his mother as he left.

"I did not do it!" Luckas shouted to her.

"What are you talking about?" he heard her say.

Then, he heard her screaming, the guards shouting.

As he fled, Luckas thought of the one person who might help him. He headed to the councillor's room, which he entered without knocking. "Forgive my intrusion. I need to speak with you," whispered Luckas.

The room was lit only by a small candle placed on the table. When Luckas' eyes adjusted, he saw a body in a kneeling position next to the bed, as if in the act of prayer. As he drew closer, Luckas observed to his horror that the man had the hilt of a small sword protruding from his back. Whoever had used it, however, had not finished the job. He was dying, but he was still taking gasps of breath.

"Luckas..." he gasped. "You must ... find ... the document."

"What document?"

"Your father ... he signed it ... then hid it in ......" The councillor couldn't finish. His last breath left his body.

Luckas slumped by the councillor's dead body. He felt utterly lost. How was he to get out of this mess? The one person who could have helped him was now dead next to him.

Then it dawned on him. Benjamen was the killer. He had killed Father and he had followed it up by murdering the councilor. His motive was all too clear. He wanted Luckas out of the way, so that he could assume the throne.

The only thing Luckas knew he had to do now was find the document. But where was it?

Luckas' thoughts were interrupted by the sound of soldiers' footsteps. Realizing that time had now run out, he darted from the room. Using secret corridors and paths, including underground chambers and wine cellars, he managed to leave the castle without being noticed.

From there he went as fast as he could to the forest, letting the trees enfold and conceal him in their embrace. From within the safety of the lowering branches, he stared at the south entrance of the kingdom. Sad and alone, he had nobody to talk to, no one he could go to for help. Everyone would believe he was the murderer now. Realizing tears were not going to do any good, he wiped his face with his sleeve, turned around and walked deeper into the forest.

Luckas knew he wouldn't be able to survive without shelter and sustenance, so he began to search for edible plants, just as Ahron had taught him in the distant past. He ended up deep in the forest, where the air was damp, the soil moist. He spotted a small formation of rocks, in the centre of which there was a pool fed by a trickle from a small river on higher ground whose stream found its way through the rocks and disappeared into the earth. He followed it upwards, where he found a spot where the water ran fast. This would be safe to drink so he quenched his thirst with the cool, translucent water.

Not far from his drinking spot, Luckas spied a cave. All he could see was a hole in a rock, and without a torch he couldn't tell if it was the home for a wild animal. Finding courage, he took a stone in one hand and a stick in the other and entered the cave. The deeper he went, the darker it became until he couldn't see the stick, although he could hear it as he tapped the ground and the walls. A few more steps and he was relieved to find that he had reached the end of the cave and had found nothing on the way. The cave was his home now.

Without any means for catching and killing wild animals, the young prince began to accept the fact that he would only be eating plants while living in the forest. However long he was there to stay he would have to forage for fruit, berries, plants, mushrooms and fronds.

He started the search at first light, then, having stored the back of the cave with what he'd found, he attended to the front. He tore branches with their leaves from nearby trees to cover the entrance, creating not only a camouflaged portal but also a makeshift door to prevent any unwanted predators from disturbing him during his sleep.

When Luckas had finished these tasks, he sat against the trunk of a tree and tried to think of a way out of his dilemma. Somehow, he had to infiltrate the castle and find the document. Entering in disguise wasn't an option; his brothers' guards would be on high alert, prepared for such a tactic, inspecting everyone and everything that entered or left.

His greatest concern was how his wife, mother and younger sister were doing, but as he thought of his family, it began to occur to him that there were three people that he might be able to trust enough to help him: Cyrenius, his Aunt Istha, and Rebekah. However, Cyrenius would probably have been informed of his father's death. He might believe Benjamen's story.

That left just two people.

As the days went by, Luckas' loneliness increased. Every day he walked towards the edge of the forest and stared at Norandia from a safe distance, wondering what people were saying about him, worried that he would never find his way home again.

33

After seven nights in the cave, Luckas decided that he had been waiting long enough and gathered all he could for the journey. He was determined to travel the long distance, even if it meant dying in the attempt. But just as he was preparing his provisions, he was disturbed by the sound of horses' hooves heading in his direction. Luckas knew there were no wild horses in the forest, so fearing for his life, he dropped everything and ran as fast as he could. But it was too late. Three men on horseback blocked his way, forcing him to take a right turn. He managed to avoid them, but there were four other riders behind him, gathering speed and closing the distance. He couldn't outrun them. His only chance was to find safety somewhere.

"Prince Luckas! Wait!" It was a familiar voice.

He tried to take another turn, but again his path was blocked.

"Luckas! Wait!" It was Seff.

"Alright!" The young prince said as he stopped. "But I did not do it!"

"We know," said Kristal. "We have not come here to capture you. We are here to join you."

"But I have been accused of murder! Why would you want to do that?"

"Can you prove you didn't do it?" Yosef asked, crossing his arms in front of him.

"Not without a document that the councillor told me to find."

The prince decided not to say any more, not until he could trust them. Their horses were blocking his way. If they decided to arrest him and return him to the castle, he was lost for sure. He felt trapped as his eyes darted from person to person, trying to discern their motives.

After a tense silence, they all dismounted and walked towards him.

"We serve only you now," Seff said as they knelt around him.

"How can this be?"

"Benjamen told us that you were responsible for the death of the king, but what he did not know was that your father had already made us promise that we would protect you if anything should happen to him."

"You took your time!"

"We ask for your forgiveness, but your brother has reinforced all entrances to the kingdom, so we had to plan a secret way out, one that would not lead to casualties among our soldiers. Now we are here, we will stay with you until you are established as the rightful king."

"But you will be accused of being traitors for helping me?"

"We know," they all said in one accord.

"I do not have enough food to feed you all," Luckas said, feeling more at ease. "We will need to gather more."

The knights rose and set off on a search.

Left alone with Seff, Luckas asked, "What is happening inside Norandia?"

"At first, there was great grief about your father. Then Benjamen added to their mourning by announcing that you were the murderer and that he would pay any informer who told him of your whereabouts. Before long, he will be crowned king, being the oldest son."

"I thought that's what might happen," Luckas said with a sigh. "How are Abigail, my mother, Shanna and the rest?"

"Lisha tried to meet with your mother twice, but both times your brother intercepted her, so she was not able to tell her anything. Abigail is not allowed to leave the fortress. Your sister is confined to her room, and the guards and soldiers from your fortress, who are now scattered all over the kingdom, have been replaced by Benjamen's men."

"Who can we ask for help?"

"That's going to be difficult. Many messengers have been sent to neighbouring kingdoms. They have been told that you murdered the king. They have determined to kill you if you are seen in their territories."

"What about Rebekah, Aunt Istha, Cyrenius?"

"We could try to reach your sister or aunt, because they have not yet agreed to your brother's petition. The only problem is that we would have to travel through several kingdoms that have sworn loyalty to your brother, and you know what that means."

"And Cyrenius?"

"Forget any idea of seeing him. He has promised to hand you over in exchange for the life of his daughter."

While they were talking, Kislon and Tytus had been collecting pieces of wood to prepare a fire to roast the deer that the other knights had just hunted and killed. Luckas watched the growing flames, pleased that he was no longer alone, comforted with the presence of the knights. The task ahead was going to be difficult, but that didn't bother him anymore; he was in the company of the men and women whom his father had trusted.

That night, as they tucked into the succulent flesh of the beast,

Luckas and Seff tried to devise a plan to enter the kingdom while the others secured the outskirts of their camp.

34

With the knights out of the picture and nobody to stop him, Benjamen decided that it was time for him to be named king of Norandia. To celebrate such an occasion, he declared a day of festivity, which all his supporters welcomed with excitement. Some of the villagers didn't agree with what was happening, but there was nothing they could do about it. The king had declared that the taverns were going to be handing out the free food and drink which he was going to supply. The announcement made the owners unhappy, but they had to obey orders if they didn't want to be taken to prison.

There was division amongst the villagers, and whilst the majority thought it was a good idea to celebrate Benjamen's coronation, others thought that he was being irresponsible. In the villages there were two kinds of people, those who danced to the rhythm of the music, and those who watched in disgust, wishing that sooner or later they would wake up from their bad dream. Many joined in with the merrymaking, but when night arrived everything went quiet, for they had all gone back to their homes to sleep.

The following day, everything returned to normal, but they didn't expect what the new king was about to announce. He had received such a good report from the previous day that he was going to proclaim another celebration that would last a full week. The people could do as they wished - work to pay their bills or join in with the festivities. They chose the latter. Benjamen thought that making everyone happy was far more important than taking care of the kingdom's affairs, so he followed his own instincts rather than listening to his advisors.

The festivities started at sunrise and finished at sunset, giving plenty of time for the villagers to drink and dance their days away. At the end of the day, the streets were full of drunken people who couldn't find their way home and ended up sleeping out in the cold. There were bodies lying everywhere, but it didn't seem to trouble Benjamen.

Day after day, there was a new party in Norandia, and the first week was soon followed by another one, that being the beginning of many more. Jakob saw that the kingdom's funds were decreasing, and fearful of seeing the kingdom plunge into poverty, he recommended his brother do something about it. Benjamen agreed; he increased the taxes of the villagers to subsidize the many parties he was planning. Some were able to pay the increase, but others had to work harder to make up the deficit.

By the end of the first month, the king was forced to buy merchandise from the neighbouring kingdoms to be able to continue providing the food and drink he had promised, causing Norandia´s coffers to diminish even further. Jakob was enjoying the parties, but he soon realized that something else would have to be done to solve the problem. Markus, meanwhile, was starting to wonder whether his brother was fit to reign; he was becoming annoyed with all the complaints that he was receiving from his villagers. He agreed that something had to be done, but he never had the courage to speak with his brother about the matter, for he knew that if anyone confronted Benjamen about it, he would not think twice in sentencing him to prison or even death.

As time went by, the kingdom's reserves were falling at an alarming rate, and once again Benjamen raised the taxes to pay the bills. The people were now forced to work much longer hours. Villagers were punished for complaining, so refrained from moaning about the new laws.

Instead of working one full day from sunrise until sunset, the people were now forced to work two full days each week. The villagers accepted that they had to pay the taxes, and they knew that if they worked for those two days, they would earn enough money to be able to please Benjamen, and after those days, they could join in the different parties to eat and drink as much as they wanted.

Benjamen wanted the celebrations to continue, and to do so, he carried on raising the taxes, which caused the villagers to have to work three days a week. Some villagers were becoming unhappy and downhearted with the constant increases, and they were starting to think that it was pointless to work for the benefit of others.

The unrest in the kingdom was palpable.

And it was growing.

35

Meanwhile, rumours that Luckas was in the woods on the south side of the kingdom began to spread among those who were upset with the new laws and the seemingly endless increase in taxation. These rumours were like a breath of fresh air for the unhappy villagers, who in an act of courage, gathered their families and all the possessions they could carry with them to try to meet up with Luckas. It was a painful decision to leave their homes, land, crops and animals behind, but they had to break away if they wanted to be free.

The first of these fugitives were the ones living in Luckas' part of the kingdom. They knew that their departure couldn't be undertaken in daylight, so they waited until nighttime and went to the south-west entrance, where they would have to face the guards, who by then were drunk.

"Stop!" shouted a guard, confronted by a father pulling a large cart with his wife and children on board. "What are you doing here?"

"We are going to look for hogs in the woods."

"All of you?"

"Yes, it's full moon. We will have a good hunt. And there will be more meat for the feasts."

The guard looked suspicious.

"Perhaps this will change your mind." The father grabbed a bag of silver coins. "Here, take this, and we will give you a hog when we return."

At that moment, several more carts emerged from the darkness, and several more guards rose from their sleepy and inebriated state. More bags of coins were passed to them. More promises of hogs were made. The guards moved to one side, allowed the carts to move on by, then returned to their slumber, but only after one hundred unhappy villagers had managed to leave the gates of Norandia.

However, this was just the beginning of their journey, for they still had to enter the woods, and try to find Luckas. In the darkened forest, nobody was able to find him, even under the light of the moon. In fact, it was the seekers who were the first to be found. The knights had been tracking them ever since they entered the outskirts of the forest.

"Where are you going?" asked Jaylon as he stepped from behind a tree.

"We are looking for Luckas."

"Who?"

"You do not know him? He is the prince of Norandia."

"Nobody has been following them," shouted Yosef as he appeared from the back of the group.

"In that case, follow us."

The families were taken to the knight's camp, where they knelt in front of Luckas.

"We vow allegiance to you and only you, oh Prince," they declared. "And our desire is to serve you alone, not your brothers, who are causing nothing but misery in the kingdom."

From that day on, the knights knew that sooner or later more discontented refugees would arrive, so they prepared to expand their camp. However, they also knew that more was required by way of preparation. Once the fugitives started to arrive in numbers, search parties would almost certainly follow, putting their lives, and Luckas' life, at risk. As a result, the decision was made to keep breaking camp every few days, relocating to other parts of the great forest, so that no one would be sure where they would be hiding.

"This may mean more work," Luckas said, "but it is a sensible tactic and it is for the greater good."

No one questioned the prince's wisdom.

Everyone was happy to be led by a man who was the furthest removed from Benjamen, and who had their best interests at heart.

36

In the fifth month after the introduction of the new laws, the tavern owners were sent to prison and were substituted by the king's soldiers. This was due to their constant complaining. They didn't want to carry on working; they thought that it was useless if they weren't making any profit. The soldiers were ordered to give rations of food and drink to the villagers while the parties continued.

The increase in taxation continued every two months and the villagers were perplexed with the uncertainty of it all, not knowing what kind of new demands they would have to face, and they were not happy at having to work more days to pay off their new debts, leaving fewer days for partying.

A steady flow of villagers continued to leave the kingdom, taking with them the possessions they were able to carry by night. Many families arrived at the south-west gate of the village where the discontented villagers hoped that the guards would be persuaded with several bags of silver coins to let them through. Those who were happy with the parties, and the free food and drink during the three days they weren't working, remained in the kingdom.

In the ninth month, everything changed. Benjamen heard rumours that many people had been leaving the kingdom and he was furious, especially when he learned that some of his own guards were becoming rich at his expense. The matter needed urgent attention and immediate action. That same night, he headed south with a group of soldiers to pay his men a visit.

"My Lord!" said one of the guards as he saw the king walking towards them. "We were not expecting your visit. If we had known, we would have prepared some food for you."

"With what? With the money you are stealing from me?"

"I do not understand."

"Do not lie. I have heard about your dealings with the villagers."

"No, my lord! You have misunderstood. The money we have been collecting is for you."

"Where is it?!"

"In that tent."

"Very well, since you have been honest, I will not punish you."

Just then, one of Benjamen's soldiers noticed something. "My Lord, there is a group of people heading this way."

"Excellent," Benjamen said. "Act normal," he said to the guards, "while my soldiers and I hide in the shadows behind those tents over there."

The group of villagers stopped in front of one of the guards, and after a short conversation, handed over two bags of silver coins. Just as the guards were about to let them past, Benjamen and his soldiers walked from behind the tents. "Well, well, well. What have we here?"

"My king! There is a perfect explanation for this."

"I am not interested in your lies. Soldiers, kill them all, including the guards!"

"No!" they cried as the king's soldiers drew their swords. "My lord! Please have mercy on us, we have families!"

"So do I."

The king had made up his mind and wasn't going to show compassion towards anyone. The soldiers raised their weapons and slew the guards and the villagers, finishing off any who were wounded and groaning in pain. It was a massacre. There were bloodied and dead bodies everywhere.

"Good," the king said. "Clean up this mess, and when you have finished, I want fifty of you to stay here. The rest will come back with me."

With that, Benjamen returned to the castle, where he wrote a new decree to be published the following morning. He wasn't going to allow any insubordination, so he increased the taxes to a point that caused everyone to have to work seven days a week, to be able to pay off what he was demanding back from those he called "the ungrateful villagers."

By this time, several thousand villagers had managed to escape, but those still inside the walls were condemned to be slaves for the rest of their lives, having soldiers follow them like shadows to make sure that they did their job. All their joy and happiness had come to an end. They could do nothing to change their situation, for they had no weapons or energy to fight against the king's army. By contrast, Benjamen's friends and close supporters lived in luxury and freedom.

Meanwhile, back in the forest, the number of villagers in the forest had grown so large there would be insufficient supplies to feed everyone.

The time had come.

Luckas and the knights decided to challenge Benjamen. He had done enough damage. Leaving the kingdom in his hands was no longer an option. And besides, Luckas' people needed feeding.

37

In the twelfth month of Benjamen's reign, Luckas had made the decision to challenge his brother and claim what rightfully was his. To accomplish the task of entering the kingdom, he had to try to gain the support of the fugitives in his camp, and therefore arranged a meeting to propose his intentions to them. As he stood in front of those who had left their villages to live in the forest, he noticed how downcast and sorrowful they were. They confessed to feeling ashamed at not rallying sooner to his cause.

The sun was starting to hide behind the horizon, and the people gathered in silence around Luckas. They didn't mind putting up with the conditions in the woods, but deep inside they wanted to return to the place of their birth.

"Villagers of Norandia," Luckas began. "I know you were deceived by my brother, being oblivious of his plans, but that is in the past, for you have decided to leave his domain to come to me. I want to assure you that one day you will repossess the land of our fathers…"

Luckas paused and waited for the people to calm down, for they had raised their voices in excitement and couldn't stop cheering. When the commotion was slow to cease, he lifted both his arms, and all the people fell silent.

"When we return to the land of our fathers, I will need all your help to restore the land, for it has been neglected and abandoned. Before that happens, the knights and I will try to retrieve what is ours. I am aware that we do not have weapons for everyone, but I ask some of you to join us. I cannot promise you that you will come out of this alive."

He finished his speech just as the sun vanished behind the mountains, allowing the darkness to settle over the forest, and with it, a deep silence. The cheering that had greeted his former utterance had gone. The people were quiet and reflective.

As the torches around the camp were ignited, the camp was illuminated by their warm, orange flames. Luckas could now see hands being raised. It was like a chain reaction, one volunteer encouraged the person next to him, who also lifted his hand, and in a short while all the people had their hands in the air.

Luckas was overwhelmed, proud to be the one to lead them. He lifted his fist high in the air. "Tomorrow we will take back our land!"

After the cheering subsided, the prince urged them to return to their tents to rest. Only those appointed to protect the camp remained awake.

The camp fell silent, save for the footsteps of those watching over the borders of the camp. Meanwhile, the prince observed his kingdom from a distance. It was drenched in the light of the full moon, and the stars that decorated the dark sky.

"Beautiful!" said Lisha as she emerged from the dark.

"It is."

"Is something concerning you?" she asked.

"I am worried that innocent people may die tomorrow. I just hope our plan works out. There has been enough suffering already."

"The people love you," Lisha said.

"And the plan will succeed," said Kislon as he also emerged from the trees. "We will defeat your brother Markus as soon as we enter those walls."

"And once Markus' side of the kingdom is under control," said Feliks as he too appeared, "we will head to your fortress to rescue Abigail."

More and more of the knights came forward to reassure Luckas. As they stood together, they all knew it was all going to be over soon.

"Go to your tents and rest," Luckas said after thanking them for their support. "Tomorrow, we will all need to be strong."

38

At dawn, Luckas walked out of his tent, hoping to gather the people for one last time before they headed towards Norandia. To his amazement, he didn't have to wait long, for his knights and villagers were ready for his battle orders.

"Long live the future king of Norandia!" they shouted.

While Luckas knew he had everyone's support, he spared the more senior people from fighting and ordered them to stay behind with the women and children to guard the camp.

They were short of food, but all the same everyone contributed what they could to have a light breakfast before marching to battle. Luckas' people were like a big, united family. They were laughing and sharing, knowing that they were all in this together and that they could only improve their situation if they fought and worked as a team, not allowing any minor quarrel from the past or present to separate them.

Luckas gave the signal to Seff, who straight away ordered everyone to take up their weapons and head to the edge of the forest, where they would be given more instructions.

"Listen!" shouted Luckas as he lifted high the sword which Seff had given him. "I want to remind you that we will only fight against those villagers and soldiers who confront us, leaving the rest in peace." Then he shouted, "Follow me!"

Not long afterwards, the guards positioned at the south-west entrance of Norandia saw Luckas and his knights appear from the forest and heading their way. Seeing that they were few, they laughed and prepared themselves for an easy victory. What they didn't see was that, not too far behind the knights, many villagers were following and emerging from the forest as well. When they eventually observed this, the guards looked at each other in shock. Fearing for their lives, they left to inform Benjamen, leaving the entrance free.

The villagers walking behind Luckas kept in formation, waiting to hear the next orders from their leader. The people knew that they would be no match against Markus' armed soldiers, but with the little that they had, such as swords, javelins and sickles, they were determined to do their best. When they arrived at the gates, however, they were met by no resistance. The villagers who didn't have weapons grabbed what the guards had left behind.

"Arrange the people in three columns, right, centre and left," Luckas shouted. "And on the front of each column, place those who have javelins."

Now that they were within the walls there was no turning back. Luckas had to move forward to free his people and liberate them from their slavery. He had one hope on the way, that some of the oppressed villagers would join him and his people in the conquest of Norandia.

39

To reach Markus' fortress, Luckas' makeshift army had to walk through two villages. As they marched along the road, they were surprised to see the land so neglected. It was dry, and it would require a lot of hard work to bring it back to its previous condition. Benjamen hadn't thought about this while the parties had been taking place, and now that he needed the fields to produce crops, he was lacking labourers as well.

Luckas saw the villagers stop what they were doing to rub their eyes in disbelief, hoping that what they were seeing wasn't an illusion. Some waved their hands in relief while others walked towards the marching army to kneel at their side in gratitude. They were relieved to see that Luckas had at last arrived to rescue them from their slavery. The news spread fast, and before they knew it, several young girls ran from their houses with baskets of what could have been the last flowers of the kingdom to throw at them as they advanced. Their welcome was overwhelming.

"Luckas," Seff warned. "Markus is coming this way with his soldiers. What shall we do?"

"Give the order for the left and right columns to position themselves in defensive formation, and have the middle column follow me. Shemuel, Yosef, Kristal, Tytus, Jaylon and Kislon follow me, we will meet my brother further on. Seff, if anything happens to me, you are to lead the people until Norandia is freed."

Seff placed his right fist on his chest, acknowledging that he would do as he was told with honour.

While the middle column followed Luckas and his six knights, the other two columns merged with each other and changed formation to create three defensive lines, holding their ground as they waited to see what was to happen. The column which was following Luckas advanced at a steady pace towards Markus' army, which was greater in numbers. As they continued marching, the villagers broke out of the column and covered both of Luckas' flanks and rear, protecting him on all sides except for the front. The gap between the opposing men was reducing with every step. A fight between both brothers was inevitable.

To his amazement, Markus and his men stopped. Luckas was confused. *Could this be a trap?* He looked at his knights, who were also unsure. The young prince was uncertain, but he and his men continued to march forward until they were only feet away. Then something extraordinary and unexpected occurred. Markus dismounted and knelt, as did his soldiers.

Luckas ordered his men to stop. Seeing that his brother wasn't going to offer any resistance, he carried on alone and stopped in front of him.

"What do you mean by this?"

"My brother, rightful King of Norandia, I do not wish to spill any more blood because of Benjamen's actions. He has caused much unhappiness in our father's land. Please accept my apologies and pardon my life. If you do, I will serve you and only you. My men will do likewise."

"Markus, look at me."

Markus was ashamed, but he obeyed.

"Markus, my brother, come here!" Luckas opened his arms. He knew that his brother spoke from his heart, and therefore he forgave him.

Perceiving that the two brothers were reconciled, the soldiers and villagers started cheering.

However, the young prince understood that there was no time to be wasted, so he called Seff to move with the troops to his position.

Seeing that many of the villagers were unarmed, Markus spoke. "Luckas, you know that in my fortress there are plenty of weapons for all your men. If you wish, I can give the order and my men will bring them, but in order not to waste time, two of my soldiers can lead the men who need equipping and show them where the armour and weapons are."

By then Seff had arrived with the rest of the men and was waiting for new orders.

Luckas spoke. "Seff, you will follow two of Markus' soldiers to equip the villagers who need weapons. Then, you and they will maintain your position. When you see Benjamen and Jakob heading towards me, start to advance towards the castle to rescue my mother and sister. After you have taken them to safety, you are to return to me. Remember, we will have my brother's troops between us, so wait for new orders behind their lines and keep a safe distance. Shemuel, Yosef, Kristal, Tytus, Jaylon and Kislon will continue to follow me."

The time for battle was now drawing near. At that very moment, a soldier was informing Benjamen and Jakob of the invasion. When Benjamen heard the news, he was furious and ordered his captain to prepare for war.

Meanwhile, Jakob left to head for his fortress to gather his men and send them to reinforce Benjamen's troops. He had decided to absent himself from the battle, staying with one hundred and fifty men until he knew how things were going. He wasn't willing to die for his brother's self-interest.

The news about Luckas' army spread through the villages whose people welcomed Luckas and his soldiers with excitement. Young women ran towards the advancing soldiers to throw flowers at their feet, and the men around the villages waved banners, for their liberator had returned to free them.

While marching through the villages, a soldier on horseback sent by Seff informed Luckas that several hundred soldiers had been sent to the castle from Jakob's fortress, and it appeared that the king's troops were starting to prepare for an imminent attack. In response, Luckas ordered his men to move faster, for they were running out of time.

The young prince and his troops were drawing nearer to the fortress when a volley of arrows felled ten of Luckas' men. Seeing that their future king was in danger, some of his soldiers moved forward and lifted their shields up, making a covering to protect him. The knights and the soldiers did the same, and once they were ready the young prince ordered them to move faster. The arrows continued to rain down from the battlements, but the shields managed to stop most of them, causing fewer casualties.

When they arrived at the fortress, fifty soldiers rushed from the gates, but they were no match for Luckas' troops, who advanced with a deafening shout and fought with immeasurable courage. In the mayhem, Luckas saw two soldiers dashing into the building, so he followed them, hoping that they would lead him to where Abigail was held. Behind the young prince were Shemuel, Kristal, Tytus and Jaylon, watching his back. Their footsteps echoed through the narrow corridors until they arrived at the court chamber, where they split. When they entered, they realised immediately that they had been fooled. They were in an ambush. The two soldiers they had been following were standing in the middle of the room, while at the far end there were three more soldiers and the one in the middle was holding Abigail. He held a small knife against her delicate throat and was threatening to kill her. These men weren't alone. There were three more soldiers on each side of the room, all waiting for the young prince and his knights to enter.

"Luckas!" screamed Abigail.

"Lower your swords and she will live," the soldier with the dagger shouted.

"Let her go and fight like a man!" shouted Luckas.

"Do not waste your energy my boy! You are outnumbered."

"Hand her over!" Kristal said. "Otherwise all three of you will be dead before Abigail is in Luckas' arms!" She placed her hand on the handle of her sword.

"What you are saying is impossible, woman!" answered the soldier holding the knife against Abigail's throat.

"I will kill you with my own sword," Kristal replied with a smile.

Shemuel raised his eyebrow at Kristal. He seemed to know what was about to happen, but she had pushed things a bit too far, and maybe even put Abigail in danger. Luckas didn't want his wife at risk, so he stepped forward to negotiate. Just as he did, the servant's door on the left-hand side opened. In the confusion, the men didn't see the arrow that flew straight through the soldier's hand, separating it from Abigail's throat.

"Attack them!" the man shouted, yelping with pain.

The two men either side of him didn't have time to respond. Another two arrows pierced their chests.

Kristal now ran towards the soldier she had threatened. The two men obstructing her were dispatched before she reached them as Jaylon hurled two small knives. Kristal jumped over their bodies and headed towards her adversary. Before he could react, Kristal drove her sword right through his abdomen. The man moaned in anguish, just as Luckas reached Abigail.

Shemuel moved to the left to attack the soldiers who were advancing towards him. He killed each one, then joined Jaylon to fight the last three soldiers who were no match for the two knights.

"Tytus! Jaylon! You fought well!" exclaimed Kristal.

"I think this time you went a bit too far." Tytus replied.

Meanwhile, Luckas was holding Abigail in his arms. "Abigail, are you alright? Did they harm you?"

"No."

"It is all over now," he said as he hugged her.

"My Lord," Shemuel said. "We should leave here. Your brother might be on the move."

"So be it," Luckas said, jolted from his tearful reunion.

Just as they were walking through the door, Abigail asked them to wait, as she needed to go to her room to fetch something. A few minutes later, she returned and handed her husband a long object wrapped in a brown cloth. Luckas grabbed it. It was the sword which Cyrenius had given him.

"I hid it in my room."

"Thank you," he said as he stared at the name engraved on the hilt.

With that, Luckas and his men left the chamber and, once outside, the prince gave a quick glance at his troops, waiting for new orders. He saw some of his men in need of medical attention.

"Thirty of you are to stay with the wounded, and Abigail, you are to remain with them."

At first, she refused. She didn't want to lose him again, but in the end she agreed.

With that, they marched in the direction of the seashore, where Luckas ordered his men to stand in formation until further notice. They stood still with the coast to their left as they watched their prince and his knights approach the shore. Luckas then turned and faced the sea, where he chose a spot to sit and think about what had to be done next. He held a small pile of sand and lifted it up, allowing the grains to pass through his fingers and fall back to the ground. Knowing that his brother was still far away and that it would take a while for him to arrive, he closed his eyes and focused on the waves as they crashed against the beach. The sound was relaxing, as if washing all his problems away, and as he waited, he could sense a gentle breeze picking up, stroking his skin whilst whispering its deepest secrets into his ears.

After a while, he opened his eyes and fixed them on the horizon, noticing that the line which separated the sea from the sky was no longer visible, for a fog was developing in the distance.

Could this work to my advantage? He thought.

41

Meanwhile, Benjamen's soldiers had positioned themselves in their respective columns and were now waiting until their king gave them the order to march towards his brother. As they stood to attention, Benjamen met with two men on their horses at the other side of the castle. These men were soldiers disguised as villagers, and they were going to carry out a different mission from the rest.

"Here take this," said Benjamen as he handed them an object wrapped in a brown cloth. "You know what you must do with it. Remember, you must travel outside the walls of Norandia to avoid being seen."

"Yes master."

"This should cover your costs for your journey to a distant land." He threw them a bag full of coins. The men turned around and went on their way, making sure at all times that nobody followed them as they galloped towards the north-east entrance, where they took a right turn and went along the edge of the outside wall of Norandia.

Benjamen knew that the men needed some time to reach their destination, so he stood and watched the men disappear into the distance. When he could no longer see them, he met with one of his captains, who after receiving the order raised his voice and instructed the troops to start advancing.

Benjamen was now moving at a slow pace on his horse, followed by his ten captains on their horses. Behind the captains were Benjamen's troops, consisting of two hundred soldiers on horseback, and seven columns of a thousand soldiers each, marching not too far from the men on horseback. The columns were made up of the kingdom's soldiers and the villagers who had been called to arms.

This was Benjamen's army.

It was time to end this rebellion and restore order to his kingdom.

42

When Seff saw that Benjamen and his troops had left and were far enough away, he ordered his men to follow him to the castle. Seff wanted to be with Luckas at the time of the fight, but he still had to rescue the queen and the princess, so he commanded the soldiers with him to march faster so that he would be able to reach the prince before their enemies. On their way to the castle, they met no resistance, leading them to believe that Benjamen had taken all the soldiers with him. Once inside the castle yard, Seff, followed by Lisha, Feliks and ten soldiers, entered the building, leaving behind the rest of the soldiers until they returned from rescuing the queen and Shanna.

The knights hadn't forgotten where the queen's room was, so they headed there straight away. All that could be heard along the castle's corridors were the soldiers' metal soles as they headed towards the queen's chamber. On their way there, they came across eight guards who they dispatched quickly. They reached the door and opened it without the need to be forceful, finding the queen looking out of the window.

"What is the meaning of all this manoeuvring of troops?" asked the queen, not bothering to check who was behind her.

"My Queen, your son is responsible," Lisha said. "He has returned to put an end to all the misery that has fallen upon Norandia. And we have come to rescue you."

The queen turned around in disbelief, for it had been a long time since she had heard that familiar and pleasant voice. She smiled. The time that she had hoped and waited for had at last arrived.

Realising that there was no time to spare, the queen walked across the room to open the door of her wardrobe, where, after moving a few items of clothing, she picked out the secret paper. Then, without delay, she went with Lisha and six of the soldiers to meet the rest of the men, all of whom had gone to free Shanna.

Shanna's door had three men posted outside who didn't hesitate in attacking Seff, Feliks and the other soldiers. Intrigued by all the shouting and noises outside, Shanna opened the door, leaving a small crack through which she could peep. The fight didn't last long, and as soon as she saw two familiar faces, she opened the door wide and shouted in excitement as she walked out of the room.

"Seff! Feliks!"

"My princess!" replied Feliks. "We must hurry, for soon your brother Luckas will need our help."

"Luckas? Oh! Wait a minute!" Shanna hurried back into her room. When she returned, she was carrying her trumpet from her left shoulder, and her quiver full of arrows from her right shoulder. That wasn't all; she also carried her sword in one hand, and her bow in the other.

Once the queen and Shanna were safe, they were escorted outside, where the other two knights and the rest of the soldiers had been waiting for them. It didn't take them long to devise a plan, and as soon as they found horses for Shanna and their queen, they marched towards the position given to them by Luckas.

Luckas, meanwhile, was still gazing at the vast sea. He knew that there had already been enough unhappiness in the land, and that more death and destruction would cause even more sorrow. He wanted to avoid that at all costs.

But Benjamen and his army were now approaching.

As soon as they were in sight, Yosef went to inform the young prince. Luckas knew that there was no turning back and that the moment to face his brother had arrived, so he stood up and headed towards his horse, ordering Tytus, Kislon and a soldier to follow him. They all mounted their steeds and rode towards Benjamen. The soldier galloping next to Luckas held a pole with a white flag. Luckas' plan was to parley with his brother, and in the process determine what his true intentions were.

Benjamen still had an iota of integrity somewhere within his soul, so out of respect for his brother, he did the same and headed towards his brother with three of his captains to meet him halfway.

"Benjamen…" Luckas was trying to say when he was interrupted by his brother.

"I see that Markus has decided to join you," Benjamen said. "What do you want?"

"I am here to claim …"

"How dare you! Are you not ashamed after being the author of the king's assassination?"

Luckas scowled.

"Listen," Benjamen continued. "I will be merciful. I will allow you to leave in peace on condition that you never return."

"I will not leave. I want what was meant for me."

"Prepare then to die. You, Markus and your people!"

"Why should more blood be shed?" Luckas asked.

"I'm listening."

"Let us leave our people out of this. Let the fight be between us two alone."

Benjamen looked surprised by this suggestion.

"Just you and me, over there," he pointed to the seashore. "The winner takes the crown."

Benjamen looked at his captains. They nodded. Benjamen

smiled. In the past, when the two of them had played with swords, Benjamen had always defeated his brother, so he was confident that he could do it again. This would be an easy victory.

"You have just signed your death warrant!" he said. "I will inform my men of the duel. I will meet you there."

Once the brothers had each informed their men, they put on their armour and they set out for the meeting point.

Five captains followed Benjamen, but after a while they stopped and allowed him to continue walking another sixty feet, until he reached the seashore, which was where the fight was going to take place. Seen from a distance, Benjamen could have been mistaken for a black demon, for his armour was of different shades of black and grey. His arm shields were like scales, and his helmet, which had two small horns on the part that covered the forehead, only allowed his eyes to be seen.

When Luckas had finished informing his men his knights helped him to put on his armour. It was grey with a silver breastplate, golden shoulders and knee protectors, light grey boots and a silver helmet with a thin golden line which encircled the top. The helmet had been made in such a way that it allowed his eyes, nose and mouth to be seen, covering his cheeks, and on top of his helmet there was a longitudinal crest of short red horse hair.

Once ready, Luckas walked along the seashore and positioned himself with the sea behind him, right in front of Benjamen. Even though he was standing alone, he wasn't on his own in the fight, for Tytus, Kislon and Kristal were sixty feet away from him on his right-hand side, and behind them, at a considerable distance were his troops.

As soon as both brothers were facing each other all eyes were fixed on them, for nobody wanted to miss what was about to happen. The tension was almost tangible. The destiny of the kingdom was in the hands of the two men. No one dared make a noise.

Benjamen looked to his left, pleased when he saw that his brother's troops were no match for his. With a mocking grin, he then looked again at his brother. "Are those the only men you were going to fight me with?"

"No!" Luckas was relieved when he saw Seff and the rest of his troops positioning themselves behind Benjamen's men. "There are more soldiers behind yours."

Luckas was the one smiling now.

"Enough!" Benjamen snapped. "Fight!"

Benjamen strode with firm steps and swung his sword with such strength that he caused Luckas to lurch backwards. The king was determined not to give his crown away without a fight, so he continued his attacks, swinging the sword towards Luckas with all his might. Although the spectators watched in silence, every so often that silence was interrupted by the loud clanging of the men's swords produced as they collided.

Benjamen's anger increased with every strike aimed at his brother, who was stopping them either with his sword or his shield, until he managed to change from defence to attack, moving forward and making his brother retreat as he rained blows upon him. Benjamen frowned; he wasn't pleased with the resistance that his brother was offering.

The next moment, both brothers had their swords up high against each other, and since the force was equal on both sides, Benjamen lifted his right leg and pushed his brother away, kicking him in the stomach. Luckas lost his balance and fell to the ground, which made Benjamen's soldiers cheer. The king tried to stab his opponent in the chest, but Luckas managed to roll away, leaving his shield behind.

Seeing that his brother was now vulnerable, Benjamen launched another attack. By now, Luckas was showing signs of weariness, but he wasn't willing to give up, so he held his sword with both hands as he waited for his brother. He was concentrating so hard on blocking the swing that he didn't see the shield coming against his head. The unexpected knock made him lose balance and take a few steps backwards before he fell to the ground. The loud metal clanging noise had left him dazed.

Luckas now removed his helmet as Benjamen dashed towards him, the taste of victory already in his mouth, his supporters already celebrating their king's triumph. On the other side, Luckas' knights stood helplessly by, lamenting not being able to intervene and prevent what seemed inevitable.

Luckas was still on the ground when his brother stood above him. He was just about to lift his sword and finish the fight when Luckas kicked his brother hard in the knee and made him fall. The young prince had to move fast, so he grabbed his sword and stood up, taking deep breaths as he waited for his brother to return to his feet. Now it was the turn of Benjamen's soldiers to feel helpless, while Luckas' knights and soldiers cheered.

Benjamen left his shield on the ground and removed his helmet, just as Luckas had done. There was a look of anger and desperation in his eyes. He had not anticipated that his brother would put up such a fight.

Luckas moved forward with a loud cry and swung his sword. This did not intimidate his brother, who managed to block his attack as both swords collided in the air. Luckas then attempted to strike Benjamen on his left side, and again his brother managed to block the thrust. But then Luckas unexpectedly hit him hard in the mouth with the hilt of his sword, causing a gash on his bottom lip.

Benjamen stepped backwards in pain and took his free hand to his lips, feeling the warm and sticky blood on his fingers. He spat in fury and grabbed a small dagger which he had on the inside of his boot, and without thinking twice he lunged towards his brother.

Benjamen now swung his sword in anger, and while his brother was occupied stopping that blow, he took the opportunity to cut him with the knife on his right shoulder. He repeated this action, but this time he aimed the knife at his brother's right thigh, injuring him again. In response, Luckas pushed his brother's sword away and thrust his own sword with all his might, managing to pierce the armour and make a deep cut in his brother's arm. They both stepped backwards, showing signs of tiredness.

Benjamen grabbed a white cloth from within his armour with the intention of wiping the blood from his lips. Markus had been watching the fight all along and knew what his brother was about to do, so he informed the knights next to him. As the cloth fell to the ground, Benjamen's two hundred mounted soldiers were already on their way towards the fight and following them at a steady pace were the rest of the soldiers on foot.

Meanwhile, as the duel continued, the fog had been advancing towards the coast until it hung like a low and widespread cloud engulfing everything in its way, reducing visibility to a minimum.

"Hurry!" Yosef said. "All the soldiers with spears make two defensive lines to protect Luckas. The rest march close behind them."

"Where are the archers?!" Shemuel looked around in search of some support.

"The majority of them were ordered to stay behind with Abigail," answered a soldier.

The soldiers, sensing that it wasn't just a struggle against their enemies, but also a battle against the unstoppable fog, ran as fast as they could. All that could be seen now were two waves of armoured men heading to where the two brothers had now continued their fight.

As soon as Benjamen's troops started to advance, Seff gave the order to his men to do the same, following close behind, with the intention of attacking their enemies from the rear.

Seff didn't feel comfortable about being far away from Luckas, so he gave orders to Lisha and Ahron to lead the soldiers whilst he advanced at a faster pace. "Feliks and Tabitha, follow me! Lisha and Ahron, lead the soldiers into battle!"

"I want to go with you!" said Shanna.

"Shanna, you know that it is not safe," Feliks cried.

"Enough!" Seff couldn't afford time for discussion, so he rethought his initial orders. "Shanna, you will come with us. Feliks, escort her. Let's go!"

The three knights and Shanna galloped towards the two brothers, passing Benjamen's troops along their right flank. Seff's intentions were to reach Luckas before anyone else, in the hope that he could rescue him.

Meanwhile, the five captains and the three knights were running towards each other. Tytus made use of his bow but with no success, for the arrows were bouncing off the captains' black and thick armour.

"You have to do better than that, my friend!" Kislon teased.

"Observe and admire!" Tytus stopped, took a deep breath and aimed at one of the captains while Kislon and Kristal kept on running.

The captains, convinced that nothing was going to harm them, moved forward without taking cover behind their shields. Once the arrow was shot, it flew across the field between the knights. As soon as the arrow found one of the eye slits, it went right through, making the captain fall to the ground.

In response to the death of their comrade, the rest of the captains lifted their shields and ran in fury towards the knights. Penetrating their advancing and tightly packed rank was going to be difficult, so Kislon looked back and gave a hand signal to Tytus, who responded with a nod and started running towards him. Whilst Tytus was running, Kislon slowed down and knelt on his four limbs, making a platform from which Tytus could propel himself over the captains. As soon as Tytus was behind the captains, he grabbed his sword and stabbed one of them in the back. His shout of pain was heard by the others, who divided and headed to one knight each, balancing the fight.

In the meantime, the cloud had already arrived at the seashore and swallowed up the coast and the two brothers, for they could no longer be seen. It continued to advance and covered the knights and the captains. Not long after that, the breeze ceased, causing the cloud to stay still.

By then, the horsemen had managed to gain ground and had entered the fog, but once inside they had to slow their pace, for they couldn't see far ahead. Then the men with spears entered, disappearing from the sight of their colleagues behind them.

Visibility inside the fog was very limited. A deep silence reigned, which was interrupted every so often by the shout of a soldier groaning in pain, and by the sound of swords clashing.

Before Seff, Tabitha, Feliks and Shanna entered the fog, they connected each horse together with a rope. They moved forward towards the sea, and when they heard the splashing of the water produced by the horses they turned to the left in search of Luckas. As they moved on, Shanna heard an agonising scream accompanied by a mournful shout.

Fearing for her brother's life, she grabbed her trumpet and blew it with all her might.

43

The sound of the trumpet echoed throughout the battlefield, reminding the soldiers and the villagers of those better times when King Staffan reigned in peace and watched out for their wellbeing. The sound couldn't be ignored back then and wasn't going to be ignored now either, so everyone stopped what they were doing and waited for the new command to be given.

Nobody knew how long the cloud was going to remain, so they just waited until the fog lifted. Those inside the mist could feel the damp air, but those outside the cloud were starting to feel the sun beating down on them and were becoming hot and anxious. There was no breeze to move the fog away, so it stayed on the coast for a while, testing the patience of the people. The waiting was long, but the people didn't mind, for deep inside their hearts they wanted to avoid the battle.

At last, a sea breeze started to blow the fog away, and as it retreated, the people who had been engulfed by it could be seen again - first the men with spears and the horsemen, then the dead bodies lying on the ground, then the knights and the remaining captains, and finally, one of the brothers.

At first glance, the people wondered who the man was sitting on the sand gazing at the sea, but as they saw the colours of his armour, they realized that it was Luckas, whose sword had been driven upright into the sand next to him. His arms were resting over his bent knees. Not far from him, Benjamen's body could be seen lying on the sand, licked by the waves lapping against his body, carrying his blood from the shore to the sea.

Luckas' supporters shouted with joy, at last free from a tyrannical ruler. Although he had been victorious, Luckas didn't feel the same way, for freedom had come at a big price. When he heard the people celebrating, he headed towards Seff, ordering him to inform the people that any celebration should be postponed, for the king himself had died, and it was fitting for them to mourn.

Meanwhile, the other side of the kingdom, one of Jakob's spies ran as fast as he could to inform his master that his brother Benjamen had died at the hands of Luckas. Jakob panicked and ordered his one hundred and fifty men to follow him. He thought that he and his brother had done much damage to the kingdom, and instead of asking for forgiveness, he had decided to escape with his men. They collected everything of value and mounted their horses, leaving the fortress empty as they galloped away from Norandia to try to find refuge elsewhere.

With Benjamen dead, and Jakob nowhere to be found, Markus should have been the next in line to the throne, but he knew that his father wanted his younger brother to become the future king, so he was going to respect that. At that time, Luckas' main priority was to restore the kingdom, so he agreed that his mother should reign as queen regent in his absence.

Luckas now had to calculate the extent of the damage and the cost of restoring Norandia. To do this, he rode on horseback throughout all the villages, and different parts of the land. Norandia was in a miserable state, and to restore it was going to take longer than expected. The villagers agreed to help him, and in exchange he promised to lower the taxes. It was going to be a slow process, but the prince had high hopes.

Inside the great walls of the Kingdom of Norandia, the land was brown and dusty with only a few green patches. The view was no longer colourful and alive, and the dullness of the land was reflected in the character of the people. Furthermore, the fields allocated for the crops had been neglected, and they were dry and full of cracks, making it difficult for anything to grow there. In the villages, the streets needed to be cleaned and repaired, as well as the homes and shops, for some had been abandoned for a long time and had wooden beams falling from the roofs. It was distressing to see that some houses had been burnt down, which meant that the families who had lived there had lost everything. The sight was heart-breaking, and many villagers tearfully lamented their loss. To make matters worse, Benjamen had also closed the kingdom's frontiers during the latter part of his reign. Consequently, the people had been forced to rely on their own resources. They possessed enough to keep them going for a while, but Luckas knew that these would soon run out. As soon as he could, he started to renew relationships with the neighbouring kingdoms by sending out emissaries to establish new trade deals.

All the while, the prince organized the workload in such a way that it didn't cause a burden to the people, and by doing this, they all worked in one accord on the reconstruction of Norandia. Each family was ordered to work on their own properties, and once they had finished, they had to move on and help their neighbours. It was good to see young and old working as a team. While some hammered the beams together, others helped in cleaning the area, taking all the rubbish away. None of this would have been possible on an empty stomach, so the wives, helped by others, made sure that everyone had a warm and tasty meal after a hard day's labour.

Once their own homes were repaired, the villagers moved on to fixing public places within their own villages, such as marketplaces, taverns, public squares and walls. The kingdom was changing day by day as they repaired or rebuilt what their forefathers had constructed many years ago.

Luckas knew that at this stage the kingdom was vulnerable, so he distributed part of his army among the four gaps in the great walls of the kingdom. The guards camped at each entrance; while some were on duty, others rested until it was their turn to do the same. This meant that while the villagers were working on the restoration of the kingdom, the guards were ensuring that nobody entered to disturb them. In addition, the prince raised several patrols that walked within the walls of Norandia, making sure that no disputes erupted.

Not long after the houses and taverns had been rebuilt, the boats were back at sea throwing their nets out to catch the fish. New merchandise was arriving by boat and by land, and the villagers soon reopened their shops and taverns, and started to trade and make money, improving the economy. It didn't take them long to start exporting their own products, and by the end of the twelfth month things were back to normal.

The signed and sealed document, which the king had left with his queen before he died, decreed that if anything happened to him his position should be transferred to his son Luckas, for he knew that Benjamen couldn't be trusted with such an honour. Luckas therefore became king and ruled the kingdom with his wife from his fortress, and his mother Ysabel and sister Shanna lived in the main castle. Benjamen's and Jakob's fortresses couldn't be abandoned, so they were occupied by trusted servants and soldiers who looked after the buildings, keeping the king informed about what was happening there.

Markus continued to live in his fortress, and one of his major tasks was to cultivate the land, which still needed a lot of attention. In the beginning, Markus and his soldiers were labouring on the dry and desolate earth, but one by one the villagers went over to help them, and after a few days of hard work the land was ready to receive the seeds.

It seemed that life was beginning to return to normal.

44

However, the peace didn't last very long, for something terrible happened, causing the queen to be upset. She had searched and ransacked her room with no success, and the more she searched the more upset she became. Her jewellery, which consisted of several golden necklaces with precious stones such as rubies, sapphires and emeralds, her matching earrings, her golden rings and many more items had been stolen and couldn't be found anywhere. Most were gifts from Staffan and her mother, so they also had an important sentimental value to her. Something had to be done about it, and fast.

At first, this was only known by the queen, her closest relatives, the knights and the people within the castle. Everywhere had been searched, from the queen's quarters to the servants' dormitories, and then this was extended to the villages. Luckas chose several men whom he trusted and sent them to find the queen's jewellery. These men searched the villages one by one. They interrogated the people, and when nothing was found, they moved on to search the fortresses. Only then, when their assignment had been completed, were the soldiers allowed to return to the castle.

The people in the villages were upset by these searches. All they could do was observe in despair as the soldiers entered their homes to look for what these villagers had denied was in their possession.

"This is absurd!" shouted a villager. "We did not steal the jewellery!"

"Sir, we have an order, and I will carry it out, with or without your consent."

"What happens if I say no?"

"We will arrest you and still search your home. So, step to one side so that my men can enter your home and search it."

The villagers knew they could do nothing, so most allowed the soldiers to enter their homes with no resistance, but there were cases where some offered resistance. In those cases, the soldiers surrounded the home and waited, for at some point they would have no more food and would have to surrender.

On the seventh day of the third month since the searches began, a decree was announced in all the villages, letting everyone know that the queen's jewellery had been found, but the people were unhappy, so they headed towards Luckas' fortress to ask for an explanation. The guards and soldiers from the kingdom were ordered to encircle Luckas' fortress, which caused the villagers to encamp behind the protective line until their petition was heard.

Luckas arranged a meeting with twenty people as witnesses, as well as the spokesmen from each village. The people were escorted to the courtyard in the fortress for the meeting, but before they could enter, they had to be searched to make sure that they weren't carrying any weapons.

In the courtyard, was a small wooden platform where Seff, Luckas, Shemuel, Abigail and Kristal stood. On the ground in front of them, acting as a protective line, were some of the guards and the rest of the knights, who were vigilant and observant to protect the safety of the king.

The people stood in front of the platform and asked for further information about where the jewellery had been found, and who was responsible. The spokesmen were in the front line, and behind them stood the other villagers.

"My lord", said a spokesman, "your generosity is remarkable, and you have always made sure that we have had all that we needed, but we would all like to know who caused such an enormous amount of turmoil within the kingdom."

"Yes, my Lord, this is a matter that we cannot accept until we find out what happened," said another spokesman.

"Furthermore," continued a third spokesman. "The law states that a thief should be punished for the crime he has committed, and punished by death if it is against the Royal Household, but we have not seen or heard of anyone being punished, therefore, we were wondering if his life has been pardoned, and if so, we would like to know why."

Luckas replied. "I understand your concerns and I know that the law commands that any thief must be punished, but before I can do that, I have to carry out an investigation."

"Why, my Lord?"

"I have a feeling that this person did not do it."

"But we have heard that the jewellery was found in your chambers. To be more precise, in Abigail's jewellery box!" The voice sounded familiar and came from a hooded man within the group.

The spokesmen and villagers started murmuring, turning towards each other to try and find out who it was. In the meantime, Seff stared at Luckas without blinking, for what had just been said was a secret that only a few chosen people knew about. Abigail stood calmly, but her breathing had accelerated, her eyes were open wide.

The people weren't happy and raised their voices. Seff grabbed his sword and assumed a defensive posture, letting his king know that he would protect him at any cost. The guards aimed their spears towards the villagers within the courtyard, while Luckas tried to resolve the matter.

"Listen to me!" he said. "The jewellery was indeed found in Abigail's possession, but she did not steal it."

"Are you trying to tell us that the jewellery appeared there by magic?"

"No, that is why I am investigating. We believe that my brother sent some men to my mother's quarters, stole the jewellery and placed it in my wife's chamber, to make it look like she had taken it."

"She stole it!" shouted a villager.

"No!" shouted Abigail.

"We demand her blood in exchange for all the trouble that has been caused!" shouted the mysterious man in the hood.

"Silence!" shouted Luckas.

"Death!" shouted another villager. The villagers shouted in unison, demanding that she should pay for her crime.

Luckas was filled with grief as he looked at Abigail. He was hoping that the people would let the situation pass, but that wasn't going to happen. It felt as if there was no escape. He didn't know what to do. He saw Abigail shaking her head in horror, for she knew that she was going to have to pay for a crime that she didn't commit.

The guards held their spears with a firm grip, for the villagers were becoming angrier, and were demanding an answer. The knights surrounded the platform to give extra support to the guards.

Luckas thought hard. It was true that the law demanded that if anyone was accused of stealing, and it was backed up by evidence, he should be punished, and, depending on the severity of the crime, that might mean death. He closed his eyes and uttered a deep sigh. He thought for what seemed to be an eternity, but all he could hear was the villagers baying for blood.

Abigail was trying to engage Luckas' attention, but he didn't respond, for he was immersed in his own thoughts, desperate for a solution. After a few moments, a cautious, nervous smile appeared on his face. He then opened his eyes and looked towards his wife. He knew what had to be done.

Luckas raised his arms to call for everybody's attention. The villagers stepped back and the guards relaxed.

"I am aware that the law of our forefathers condemns the act of stealing and that the penalty is death. As I have already said, I am carrying out an investigation, for I know that Abigail is no thief..."

"If that statement is true, there still must be justice!"

Luckas spoke again. "There will be justice, but the law also says that a condemned person's life can be spared when someone else, in a higher position, takes his or her place."

Silence fell upon the courtyard.

"That person will be me," Luckas said.

Seff stepped forward. "My Lord, you do not need to do this. I will fight everyone who opposes you, until my final breath."

"Seff, you have served me well, but I must do this so that the law is fulfilled. Please take good care of my wife, mother and sister."

"Luckas, what have you done?" Abigail couldn't believe her ears.

"I love you too much, my darling wife, and I do not want to see you die." Luckas hugged her as he spoke.

"Because you have offered your life on behalf of hers," said one of the spokesmen, "instead of taking you to the cage now, you will be summoned an hour before sunset."

"So be it."

The villagers and spokesmen went back to their homes to inform the people what had happened. Most were in distress, for they didn't want to see their king die, but there were some who wanted to witness his death and headed to the place of execution to gain a good view of the event.

45

The king looked at Abigail's sorrowful eyes and held her hand, trying to let her know that everything would be fine, but she couldn't avoid crying in utter despair. As he stared at her, he remembered those days in which she looked after him when he was alone, fed him when he was hungry, and dressed his wounds when he was injured. Luckas' love for Abigail was far greater than his fear of death. He would have preferred another option, but he had to follow what was established in the law long ago.

He spent his last hours enjoying the company of his family and friends. In the meantime, he also tried to sort out with his councillor the matters of the kingdom, but it was too much to do in such a short time, so he handed them over to his mother, who would have to help Abigail and walk alongside her until she could handle the matters on her own.

In the last hour, he went to his chamber, where he clothed himself with the best royal garments he had. He then grabbed the emerald stone from the window ledge and placed it in his pocket. Just before he walked out of his room he stared at the mirror. Then, as he looked into his own eyes, he gathered all his courage and smiled, believing that he was doing the right thing. He walked in confidence towards the main gate of the fortress, where ten soldiers and the spokesmen from the villages awaited him.

He could have gone on horseback to the cage, but he opted to walk towards it instead, allowing himself to enjoy the presence of his loved ones a little bit longer. Abigail was wearing a long black dress and, on his way to the cage, she begged him to find another way.

"Do not worry, my love," Luckas said softly. "It will not be long before we are together again."

Abigail was too crushed to reply.

The knights, men and women who had watched him grow from being a child, were right behind him, hoping that he would give the order for them to rescue him, but it seemed that the king had made up his mind.

There was nothing that the queen could do to convince her son to change his decision, and after crying in anguish she soon realized that there was no way around it and that her son was going to die.

Just before arriving at the cage, Luckas stopped and turned to his sister Shanna. She had grown to be a bright young woman with a strong character who almost always spoke in a straightforward manner. Crying was something she didn't like doing, for it made her feel uncomfortable, but this time, knowing that she was going to lose her brother forever, she found it hard to withhold her tears, allowing a few of them to run down her cheeks.

Luckas looked at her and bent forward, whispering into her ear a few words which caused her to hug him. In response, she stepped back and nodded as she wiped the tears from her cheeks.

Those villagers who had sympathized with Benjamen were gathered around the cage, observing every move with expectation, for they had waited a long time to see what they were about to see. Not too far from there, a man wearing a hood stood still, observing carefully what was about to happen.

Luckas gave a final hug to his mother, and then to Abigail. As he was holding her, two soldiers grabbed him and dragged him away from her. The king's hands were pulled apart from Abigail's.

The king was now escorted to the top of the cage, where a soldier who had opened the small trapdoor waited for him. As was the custom, another soldier checked his clothes to make sure that he wasn't carrying any weapons. The guard placed his hand inside one of the condemned man's pockets and pulled out the precious stone.

"For good luck!" Luckas said.

The soldier saw that he couldn't do much harm with it, so he shrugged his shoulders and placed it back in the king's pocket, then gave a nod to indicate that he had finished.

Seff climbed up the ladders and walked towards Luckas. They both stared at each other. Words at this point were worthless, for everything that had to be said had already been said. Luckas smiled and nodded, letting Seff know that he was ready. As Luckas entered the cage, the knight couldn't believe that he wouldn't see his friend and king anymore.

The spectators now watched the soldiers who were about to move the middle door which separated both sides of the interior of the cage. There was a small beam of light that came through the top door, but the moment it was closed it became pitch black. The cage emitted a repulsive and nauseating stench, the odour of imminent death. Even though Luckas couldn't see anything, he didn't allow fear to control his feelings; he had a firm pulse as he made his way through the sound of snapping under his feet. The dry bones from past thieves and murderers were breaking as he walked towards one of the walls.

The room was quiet, save for the fracturing of the remains below and the sound of his own breathing, calm and resolute. He then remembered the emerald stone and withdrew it from his pocket. At first, he could see nothing, but in a split second, as if by magic, the stone illuminated the whole interior in a bright green colour. Luckas, heading towards the far end wall, could now see clearly where he was walking. His excitement didn't last long, however, for the middle door was starting to open. Seeing this, many of the people outside the cage began to walk back to their homes, for there was nothing else to see and the king's death was now certain.

Inside the cage, Luckas stepped back against the wall. As the door opened, he could see luminous eyes ahead of him.

Wolves!

It was all over for Luckas. No matter how strong he was, he wasn't going to be able to defeat a pack of ferocious and hungry wolves.

Luckas fixed his eyes on the slowly advancing wolves, while with his hands he groped and felt along the wall. As king, he knew what was whispered to the criminals just before they entered the cage, that there were two swords hanging on the wall on which he was leaning. One was a normal sized sword and the other was smaller in size, similar to a dagger. Those were placed there for the people who entered the cage to use in self-defense. The law stipulated that if they were brave and skillful enough to escape the cage alive, their crimes would be forgiven. However, no criminal had ever succeeded. The information was conveyed to them too late for them to devise a plan to locate and use the weapons.

One of the wolves made the first move and ran towards Luckas. Just as the creature started running, the king managed to grab the sword and swung it towards the wolf's skull, killing it on the spot. He still needed the dagger, so he turned, and as soon as he saw it in the green light, he grabbed it and faced the wolves again, finding out that two of the wolves were advancing towards him.

He didn't have much time, so he aimed the sword towards the wolf that jumped at him. He thrust it forwards, piercing through the wolf's mouth and throat. As he tried to extricate the weapon lodged in the wolf's mouth, the other one attacked him from the left, not giving him enough time to retrieve his sword, so he made use of his dagger, managing to stab the wolf in its chest.

The king couldn't afford any margin for error, so after recovering his sword he scanned the situation and stepped towards the remaining wolves who were snarling angrily at him. He swung the sword and cut the face of one of the wolves, causing it to retreat in pain. He then turned and pierced another wolf with his sword and knife. Once again, he had to retrieve one of his weapons. Taking longer than expected, he was caught off guard, and a wolf bit him on his right leg. The king yelled in agony and lost his balance, but while he was falling, he managed to grab his knife and thrust it downwards into its skull, killing it in an instant.

With Luckas now kneeling, a she-wolf jumped towards him, but once again he dispatched it with a quick thrust of his sword. The wolf's limp body fell upon the king, causing him to fall backwards. He pushed the dead animal to one side. As he stood up, he realized that he didn't have time to recover his sword, so he decided to face the remaining wolves with his knife.

The two wolves, one of them injured, fixed their eyes on their prey and advanced. The injured wolf attacked Luckas on the right and dug its teeth into his right shoulder. The other wolf leapt towards his throat, but the king dodged to one side, pushing his dagger deep into the animal's neck.

As its life blood poured from the wound into its matted fur, the king grabbed the dagger, pulled it from the yelping wolf, and tore the flesh from the side of the other wolf, who howled with pain. Both creatures were dying, and the rest of the wolves were dead.

The pain in the king's shoulder was unspeakable. He needed medical attention and fast. But the light from his stone was now fading. He was running out of time.

The king managed to stand up and limp towards the other side of the cage, where he knew that he would find what he needed. He walked past the one surviving wolf, severely injured, and saw that the animal was struggling to breathe. He shuffled to the far wall, continuing his search.

Outside, meanwhile, a messenger from the queen headed towards the five guards who were watching over the cage.

"I bring wine and food from the queen."

"Please tell her majesty that we are very grateful," one of them said.

The guards opened the bottles of wine and drank heartily, feasting and enjoying the tasty banquet that they had been offered.

Inside the cage, Luckas approached the wall and found the axe that had been hanging there since the cage had been built. Once he had it in his grip, he approached the wolf and stood beside it. He looked at the animal with pity, lifted the axe and killed the animal, ending its suffering.

The light inside the cage was now diminishing, so he limped towards the stone and picked it up, aiming the remaining light towards his injuries as he covered them with strips of clothing torn from his own clothes. As soon as he finished, he aimed the light towards the walls. Many years before, his father had told him about an X which had been painted with lime on one of the walls. The X revealed which of the walls had been constructed with material that could be broken with the axe. In an act of kindness, the forefathers had positioned the axe on the wall, allowing the chance of freedom to all those who entered the cage. The reason why nobody ever managed to escape was because they had no light. Luckas, however, had the emerald stone.

When he found the X, the light that was emitted from the emerald stone vanished, and with it, darkness engulfed the cage. He placed the stone in his pocket and started hacking into the wooden wall. After several strikes, it felt as if it was giving way, allowing Luckas to look through a crack. It was night now outside. No one was around. He could escape without fear of being discovered.

Luckas was now exhausted, every strike of his axe making him weaker. The fact that he had been losing blood didn't help him either. But after several more efforts, he made a way through the wall.

He stretched his hand through the cavity in the wall. He couldn't see his hand, but he could feel the hole increasing in size as he pushed and pulled the material away. Soon he was able to fit his head through and breathe the fresh air. This gave him hope and he felt a surge of energy.

It took him a while to be able to make a hole big enough for his whole body, but when he had finished, a beam of moonlight entered the cage. He now had a way out to the outside world.

Before crawling through the hole, he grabbed the axe, sword, and dagger and wrapped them in his shirt. As he emerged, he was welcomed by the cool gentle breeze of the night. He peeped past the corner of the cage. Not too far away the guards were lying on the floor, appearing to be sleeping.

Using the cover of night, he started his long walk to the only person who could help him.

Seff.

47

The main doors of the castle were guarded, and going through them was going to prove difficult, so he headed towards a hidden door that only his father and he knew existed. This led him to a secret passage which took him to the heart of the castle, where it connected with the rest of the corridors. He knew that the people were sleeping, so he walked through the different passages without making a sound until he reached the door he was looking for. He knocked on the door in the hope that none of the patrolling guards would hear him.

Nothing happened.

It was all far too quiet and he couldn't hear any movement inside.

The king knocked again, this time a little harder, hoping that the sound wouldn't wake any light sleepers. It seemed that the person on the other side was fast asleep or wasn't in his chamber.

He knocked a third time.

This time he heard movement.

The door was unlocked and opened.

"Seff," he said, falling into his friend's arms.

"My king!"

As Luckas fainted, Seff managed to hold him up. His sword, however, fell to the floor, clattering noisily on the paved stones.

The door opposite Seff opened. Yosef, just woken, rubbed his eyes, recognized his wounded king and ran to help.

"How did he get here?"

"I do not know, my friend. Help me to lay him on my bed."

As they lay their friend on the mattress, Seff lit several candles. In their light, both knights could see how seriously their king had been wounded.

"Find Ahron and tell him what has happened," Seff whispered. "Once you have spoken with him, tell Kislon to prepare two horses. It's a clear night, but you may need torches. Also, ask Tabitha to bring some fresh water."

Yosef nodded.

"And tell no one about this and try not to be seen by the guards."

Not long after Yosef had gone, Ahron arrived with some herbs. He noticed that the king had several scratches and two bites which needed attention right away. Just when he was about to ask Seff for some fresh water, two hasty knocks followed by two slow knocks were heard at the door. Seff opened it, allowing Tabitha to enter with a bowl of water.

Yosef arrived not long after Tabitha, but he didn't stay long; Seff ordered him to go to the cage with Kislon to inspect it and find out what had happened, and if need be, to cover up any signs showing the king had managed to escape, for this could not be allowed to come to light at such a delicate time.

Just as Yosef was about to leave, a strange knock came from the other side, one no one recognized. Seff wasn't expecting anybody else, so as he walked towards the door, he told Yosef to step behind it so as not to be seen.

"Is everything fine?" said a voice from the other side.

"Hold on," said Seff as he headed towards the door to open it.

It was one of the guards. "We heard a noise," he said, "and since you are the only one who has light coming from under the door, my lord, we thought we would ask if you were all right."

"Yes, thank you… I could not sleep, so I went for a walk, and… how clumsy of me! I dropped the candle stick holder as I entered my room … Sorry for the noise…"

"Thank you, my lord. I'll return to my post."

As soon as Seff closed the door, Ahron and Tabitha started cleaning the king's wounds. Ahron used the rare herbs and ancient medicine on the injuries. Seff stood by and observed. The wounds would heal in time, but the scars would remain forever, a reminder of the king's sacrificial love for his wife.

Kislon and Yosef went to Seff's chamber just after sunrise. Ahron remained at the bedside, watching over Luckas all the time. Tabitha wanted to stay close, so she sat on the couch and waited until she was given new orders. Seff never strayed too far from the door, making sure that they wouldn't have any unexpected visitors.

"Who would believe it?" Kislon whispered. "The king managed to escape from that cage."

"I wonder how?" Seff said.

"With the axe that he brought with him last night," Yosef suggested.

"Where did he get that from?" Ahron asked. "Did he kill the wolves?"

"He must have," Seff said.

"We have covered the hole with some wooden planks," Yosef said. "The guards were drunk, so there were no problems."

"What do we do now?" asked Tabitha.

"We cannot tell anyone about Luckas," Seff said firmly.

He was about to say more when he was interrupted.

Trumpets were beginning to sound at the castle gates, signalling that someone important had arrived.

"Are we expecting someone?" Yosef asked.

Seff shook his head.

Tabitha was curious, so she walked towards the window. "It's a rider on a white horse surrounded by ten horsemen and followed by twenty soldiers on foot."

"What!" Kislon exclaimed. "News travels fast in this land."

"That, or we have traitors inside the kingdom," Yosef said.

"Tabitha, do you know who the rider is?" Seff asked.

"No, but I will find out. I just have to get closer."

Tabitha was the perfect knight for the task; stealth was one of her finest attributes. So, while she went to gather some information, the other knights waited for her in Seff's chamber.

Tabitha moved fast through the corridors and arrived at the entrance, where she waited for the mysterious man to enter. He seemed to be an important figure, but she couldn't see his face, for it was covered by a hood. His steps were firm and protecting him on both sides were four of his personal warriors. Their armour was as black as night, causing fear wherever they walked.

Tabitha followed them, hiding behind whatever offered her good cover. The mysterious man continued walking and headed towards the king's throne room, where it transpired that Queen Ysabel was waiting for him. Tabitha knew that she couldn't enter through the main door, so she took a shortcut and made use of a private door which only the knights knew about. She entered and hid herself behind the columns and the chairs, making her way forward until she knelt behind a curtain near both thrones.

"My dearest Ysabel," said the man as he removed his hood.

"Oh, it is you. What brings you here?"

"I heard about your son's death. I have come to offer my condolences. And now, I have come to claim my throne."

"You are mistaken. Markus will take Luckas' place."

"Markus and I had a good conversation last night, and he was so pleased to see me that we celebrated together. I have to admit though, we may have drunk more than we should have done!"

"What have you done to him?!"

"Do not worry my queen, for he still lives, but he is on his way to the forest with a contingent of my men. You might be thinking, how did I manage to take him out unnoticed? Well, before Benjamen died, he swapped several soldiers between his and his brother's fortress and because I knew who they were and where to find them, it worked to my advantage."

"You!"

"Now! Now! No need to be angry."

"So, what now?" demanded the queen.

"Well, just as we speak, I have a soldier running up the stairs that lead to the top of the tower, and once there he will exchange the kingdom's flag for a black one, letting my troops know that it is all clear to enter."

"My guards will stop them."

"Well..." the man was going to continue when he heard the trumpets sound. "Listen to that! Your soldiers have just been informed not to attack the incoming army."

"You must have planned this long ago..."

"You are so right, and at last I can sit on my throne. It is just a pity that Luckas had a soft heart and offered his life on behalf of his wife's."

"So, you were the one who conspired against Luckas with the theft of the jewelry!"

"I did not do it, but I know who did."

The queen slapped the man.

The man smiled as he placed his hand on his chin and gave a

nod to his soldiers, who grabbed the queen and took her to her chambers.

Tabitha ran back to Seff's chamber to give him the news.

The room fell silent.

"You are not going to believe who I just saw!" she said. "I saw the king's brother."

"You are referring to Jakob," Yosef said.

"If only that were so."

"Then who?"

"I saw Kidron."

"You are joking."

"I am not, and he is claiming the throne. In fact, as we speak his troops are entering Norandia."

"What about Markus?" asked Jaylon.

"He has disappeared. Our only hope is Luckas, but he is still weak."

As they spoke, Seff walked towards the window to see for himself what he had just heard. He couldn't believe his eyes; hundreds of soldiers were entering the kingdom and taking up their positions. Now it all started to make sense. Kidron had planned all along to take the throne.

"We must hide Luckas until he is fit to confront his uncle," said Seff.

"I think my chamber would be fine for that, as the soldiers do not dare to enter it due to my puma," said Ahron.

"Good idea."

Two of the knights carried Luckas while the rest went out into the passages to clear the way. It didn't take them long and once inside the chamber they placed Luckas on Ahron's bed.

That afternoon, Kidron met with the knights in the courtroom. He offered them the chance to stay and serve him, or else, they would have to leave and never return. The knights accepted, though deep inside they were still loyal to Luckas and were only buying their friend some extra time. That is why they had determined in their hearts that whenever they had to work alongside Kidron's generals, they would only give them the information they needed to know.

As soon as Kidron set foot in the castle, he made sure that everything he had planned for worked out with exact precision and without delays. He used the first day to find out who was going to follow and serve him. On the second day, he established his personal councillors and went through all the paperwork that he needed to go through to establish Norandia as his kingdom. All the while, the queen was kept in her quarters with her daughter Shanna, only being summoned if he demanded their presence. Abigail was also under surveillance in her chambers.

To finish his master plan, at the break of dawn on the third day, Kidron announced that that same night he was going to be named king. The coronation was going to be a public event in which he required the presence of all the spokesmen and generals to be witnesses. His list of petitions didn't end there, for he also requested that the people would be outside the castle courtyard to cheer him when he walked through the main door.

While the preparations for the ceremony were taking place, Luckas was still recovering and unaware of what was happening. Some of the knights were becoming anxious, for they knew that if he found out, Kidron would give orders to kill him. These knights had to be present at the ceremony, so they went with the intention of delaying it in the hope that they could buy some time.

Some of the guests, such as spokesmen, lords and several villagers, had already started arriving and were sitting on the best seats to see the ceremony. The throne hall had been decorated just as Kidron wanted, with three thrones placed at the end facing all the benches. The columns were adorned with purple and yellow flowers, and because it was going to be dark soon, the room was lit with hundreds of candles, whose light penetrated even the most hidden corners of the hall.

Not knowing who he could yet trust, Kidron placed sixty soldiers inside the throne hall. They were standing around the benches and next to what would be his throne. He also placed an extra twenty soldiers, without the knights' knowledge, in another room that was concealed by a long red curtain behind the thrones. From the ceiling hung four flags - a black one for his past life, a purple one for royalty, a red one for death, and a golden one for the new period of his reign.

As all this was going on, Ahron and Feliks paced in their chamber, wondering how the ceremony was going. This chamber led to a spare room which had a door onto a spacious balcony from where there was an extensive view of the kingdom. As Luckas was starting to wake up, they headed there.

"I wish we could have mentioned that Luckas is still alive," Feliks said.

"You know as well as I do," Ahron said, "that if the news had reached Kidron's ears, he would have searched for him and killed him. We are still not sure where Luckas obtained the axe and those swords when he was in the cage. If he finds out, I am certain that Kidron will not allow him to go in there again."

"I wonder how the ceremony is going?" Feliks said.

"I have not heard the trumpets," Ahron said, "so I assume that he has not been named king yet. It is a pity that Luckas is not there to stop the coronation."

"What was that?" Feliks had heard a door slamming.

They both rushed into the chamber to find that Luckas was no longer lying on the bed. In a panic, they searched the rooms but there was no trace of him.

"So much for having a puma," remarked Feliks.

"Do not blame it on my puma," Ahron said. "If it had been an intruder, she would have attacked him, but she has known Luckas since he was a child, so she had no reason to attack him."

"Who will tell Seff?"

"I will!"

"Where do you think Luckas has gone?"

"I do not know, but we should start searching for him."

Ahron and Feliks grabbed their swords and rushed out from the chamber, hoping that they would reach Luckas before any of Kidron's soldiers discovered him. They decided not to split up and to keep together all the way, thinking that they would have a better chance of defending him in the event of having to fight against anyone who crossed his path.

49

Everyone in the throne room fell silent as the court herald knocked on the floor three times with his golden stick, letting the people know that the new and future King of Norandia was about to enter.

Kidron arrived wearing a golden robe with a white tunic, looking joyful about what was about to happen. He held a golden goblet in his left hand, sipping from it when it pleased him. As he walked along the red carpet, two soldiers followed him, holding a chain which was tied around Ysabel's and Abigail's waists. The two women weren't just being pulled by the soldiers in front of them; they were also being pushed by another two walking behind them. They wore black dresses, for they didn't agree with this ceremony, but Kidron didn't mind, for it made his outfit stand out more.

Kidron sat on the throne, and Ysabel was forced to sit on his righthand side, Abigail on his left. To make sure they didn't escape, they had both been tied to their thrones. They were sad and in pain, not wanting to be there, but they were compelled to, and could do nothing about it.

To make Kidron believe that he could trust them, the knights didn't do anything to ease either of the queens' distress. Shanna had been given more freedom, for she was sitting untied on the front bench.

The ceremony started as soon as Kidron and the two women sat down.

While things progressed inside, footsteps could be heard outside the throne room. The four sentries guarding the door looked at each other, wondering who it could be, as there was an embargo on people walking about within the castle grounds.

The steps became louder and louder.

The sentries didn't want to interrupt the ceremony, so they decided that two of them should investigate. Norandia's soldiers had been combined with Kidron's. The two soldiers who stayed at the door were Kidron's personal guards, while the other two were Norandia's.

When they walked around the corner, the two Norandian guards couldn't believe their eyes when they saw who it was walking towards them.

They knelt and bowed their heads to the ground, allowing the man to walk past them unchallenged.

Luckas continued to the door of the throne room, his bow and arrow in his hand. He knew that the other two soldiers wouldn't hesitate to oppose him, so he shot twice as soon as he saw them, wincing with pain at the pressure on his injured shoulder. As he strode forward, the two arrows struck the two soldiers, killing them at once.

Luckas stopped just in front of the door. He put an arrow on the bow as he took deep breaths.

There was no turning back now.

The other two guards wanted to support him and had now caught up with him. They stood right behind Luckas.

Meanwhile, Kidron was sitting on the throne and waiting for the priest to proclaim him king.

A few moments later, the trumpeters welcomed the entrance of the priest who walked towards Kidron. He then stood behind the throne, took the crown from a nearby table and lifted it. Before placing the golden object on Kidron's head, he said some words.

"We are about to greet the new king, but before we do, I must ask the question. Is there anybody present who is against this coronation?"

Outside, Luckas said nothing. He looked at the two guards and gave them a nod, letting them know that he was ready.

The doors opened, revealing Luckas with his bow and arrow directed towards the bearded man sitting on his throne. His suspicions were confirmed; it was his uncle, who after several attempts was about to take possession of what he coveted so badly.

"Uncle! You have been sentenced. The verdict is death!"

Luckas released the arrow.

The entry had caught everyone by surprise, not least Kidron. It took a few seconds for Kidron's soldiers to process what was happening, but when they had, they ran towards Luckas. Five soldiers encircled him, pointing their spears at his neck. He was trapped and he wasn't the only one, for even his knights were surrounded by Kidron's soldiers.

Luckas looked at Shanna and gave her a nod, letting her know that it was her turn. She understood in an instant what he meant, and because nobody was watching over her, she was able to hold the silver trumpet hanging from her neck and blew it with all her strength. The unusual and deep sound reverberated within the castle walls.

A captain slapped her on the face and pulled the trumpet away from her as he pushed her to the ground.

"My lord, everything is under control," said the captain. "What would you like us to do with them?"

There was silence from the throne.

Kidron wasn't answering, so the captain turned his head towards his king, who was still holding his goblet which was tilted and tipping out its contents.

Kidron was dead, and the red wine was pouring like blood onto the floor. The arrow had pierced his skull and had killed him.

Without a king, the captain barked his orders. "I am in charge here now. Take the prince outside and kill him, and do the same with the knights, for they are traitors!"

"You might want to think that through," Seff said with a smile.

"Why?"

"You recognise the trumpet you have in your hands?"

"What about it?"

"It has been blown, and very soon you will have all the Norandian guards and soldiers descending upon you, and because Luckas is alive, they will fight and defend him to the last."

"You are bluffing."

At that moment, two of Kidron's soldiers entered the room in a rush. "My lord!" shouted one of the soldiers as he looked at the throne.

"He cannot answer," the captain said.

"Captain, we are being attacked by hundreds of soldiers and farmers. It is impossible to hold them back! What shall we do?"

The captain looked away from the messenger and checked his surroundings, noticing that there was no way out. He then turned to the knights and saw them fighting with his men. He knew it was soon going to be all over. He dropped his sword. "Let the trumpeters announce our surrender," he shouted.

The Norandian guards made their way to the hall and arrested Kidron's soldiers. In the meantime, Luckas walked towards his throne. Ordering the removal of his uncle's body, he took his rightful place. He sat down and looked at the court herald, who knocked on the floor twice with his pole.

Luckas stood. "We all know who this man was - my uncle, my accuser and the one behind my father's death. He has paid for his crimes, as will those who follow him. As for his soldiers, I will allow you to leave in peace, never to return, but if at sunrise you are still found to be within the kingdom, you will be sentenced to death. Now, as son of Staffan I will rule over Norandia, and it will be just as it was intended to be right from the beginning, taking my father's place and re-establishing all that he did. All those who want to follow me are welcome to stay. The rest will be treated as traitors."

The people had been quiet while he spoke, but that didn't last long, because as soon as he finished, the silence was broken by people kneeling and bowing. Seeing that everyone accepted the situation, the court herald shouted a few words which everyone repeated with a shout of joy.

"Long live Luckas!"

"Long live Luckas!"

"Long live the King of Norandia!"

"Long live the King of Norandia!"

Luckas sat on his throne, looked at Abigail and held her hand with a firm grip, assuring her that she wasn't seeing a ghost. The queen looked at her son and smiled, showing that she was proud of him, and Shanna, happy to see her brother, ran towards him to hug him.

It took some time after that for Norandia to return to the way it once had been. All those who didn't agree with Luckas being king left the kingdom, and there was nothing that Luckas could do about it, for they had made their decision. That was just a minor part of the story, however, for there were still many matters in need of Luckas' attention, which he started to deal with as soon as he took control of the kingdom's affairs. He wanted to rule so that the people were no longer fearful, but he also didn't want them to forget what their king had endured because of his love for his wife and his kingdom. For this, he ordered that the cage be cleaned, repaired, and left as a monument to sadder times.

As King of Norandia, Luckas moved into the castle with Abigail, allowing his mother to stay with them, and he donated his fortress to his sister Shanna, who was delighted to take on the responsibility.

The knights also stayed in the main castle, and part of their assignment was to train apprentices so that in due course they too would become the king's knights. On completion of their training, they would be sent to the different fortresses throughout Norandia.

Some time passed when Markus at last managed to return to the kingdom. The soldiers who had held him captive set him free immediately they heard about what had happened to Kidron. Markus knew how to move about in the forest, so once he knew where he was, he headed back home, where he swore loyalty to his brother, the new and rightful King of Norandia.

One day in the months that followed, Luckas was standing on his balcony contemplating his kingdom. He knew he had gone through a lot, but it had been worth it, as now he was able to continue the legacy his father and forefathers had left. From where he was standing, everything seemed to be at peace, for the people were living in harmony as they attended to their daily affairs. There were no longer large companies of soldiers travelling throughout the kingdom, just the right amount to ensure the safety of the people.

While standing there, a gentle breeze brushed his skin and seemed to whisper into his ears what his father and he himself had waited for so long to hear, that there was peace in the land.

As he stood there, he felt a hand on his back which then slid around his right side until stopping at his chest.

It was Abigail. She kissed his neck while placing her left arm around his waist. "Luckas?" she said.

"Yes, my love?"

"I am so happy that you are back."

"So am I. At one point, I really didn't think I was going to make it."

"But you did. And I am glad, not only for myself but for …"

She took her hand from Luckas' stomach and placed it on her own.

"Abigail?!" Luckas said, gasping.

"It is true," she said. "I am with child!"

THE END

Names and their meanings

Name: Staffan
Gender: Male
Meaning: Crown

Name: Ysabel
Gender: Female
Meaning: Oath of God

Name: Rebekah
Gender: Female
Meaning: Beautiful, captivating

Name: Benjamen
Gender: Male
Meaning: Son of the right hand

Name: Jakob
Gender: Male
Meaning: Supplanter, to follow

Name: Markus
Gender: Male
Meaning: A defense

Name: Luckas
Gender: Male
Meaning: Bringer of light

Name: Shanna
Gender: Female
Meaning: Gracious gift of God

Name: Kidron
Gender: Male
Meaning: Turbid, black stream

Name: Istha
Gender: Female
Meaning: Star

Name: Ruphus
Gender: Male
Meaning: Red-haired

Name: Cyrenius
Gender: Male
Meaning: Warrior

Name: Salwa
Gender: Female
Meaning: Calm, peaceful

Name: Davian
Gender: Male
Meaning: Beloved

Name: Abigail
Gender: Female
Meaning: Source of joy

Name: Lisha
Gender: Female
Meaning: Oath of God

Name: Shemuel
Gender: Male
Meaning: God hears

Name: Jaylon
Gender: Male
Meaning: Supplanter, to follow

Name: Ahron
Gender: Male
Meaning: Mountaineer, mountain of strength

Name: Seff
Gender: Male
Meaning: Wolf

Name: Tytus
Gender: Male
Meaning: Honorable

Name: Feliks
Gender: Male
Meaning: Happy

Name: Tabitha
Gender: Female
Meaning: Gazelle, small deer

Name: Kristal
Gender: Female
Meaning: Ice, rock

Name: Kislon
Gender: Male
Meaning: Hopeful, confident

Name: Yosef
Gender: Male
Meaning: God will increase

Contact the Author

contact.miguel.tf@gmail.com

Printed in Great Britain
by Amazon

51418786R00154